WICKED HOPE

THE DEVIL'S DEAL

ELIZA RAINE

For those who struggle to believe.
Never give up.

ONE

"Ouch!"

Dull pain throbbed through my side as Rory landed another blow to my ribs.

"Pay attention, newbie." She darted out of reach before my reactive kick could find its mark.

"It's kind of hard to concentrate," I grumbled.

"Look, you asked for these lessons." She straightened, her defensive movements from foot to foot stilling. "I'm not wasting my time, am I?"

"No. Of course not. I'll focus, I promise."

Rory nodded and dropped her weight again, raising her gloved fists.

This was our fourth self-defense class since Banks had beaten the shit out of us both at Ward HQ, in as many days. And I *was* getting better.

But I also had a good reason for struggling to concentrate.

I had been so certain that the voice I had heard on Malc's radio recording had been my mom's.

We had been through every inch of the building, Nox using his considerable influence and pissing off a number of people, including his brother Michael, but we found no trace of her. Or anyone who even recognized her picture.

Make sure she finds nothing.

That was what the voice on the radio had said. About me, looking for my parents.

Did they leave me on purpose?

I felt my lip curl as I threw a hard punch at Rory. She ducked easily, landing a counter-blow on my arm as she rose. I aimed a low kick at her, catching her knee and making her skip backward.

"Nice," she said, begrudgingly. "Water."

I was relieved to drop my arms to my side and catch my breath as she turned and strode to the bench hosting our water bottles, and Francis. We were out in the gardens at Lavender Oaks, and I couldn't help smiling at Francis' enthralled face.

"Honey, the water bottle just vanished here." She waved at where Rory's stuff was. "Does that mean she picked it up?"

Rory scowled at Francis and chugged from her bottle.

"Yes," I told her. "Rory is standing right next to you."

Francis let out a long breath. The Veil hadn't been lifted for her, so although she believed me, one hundred percent, that I was sparring with a pixie, she couldn't see Rory. "It sure is funny watching you fight on your own. It's like that movie."

"Honestly, they let you watch anything here," I said, shaking my head.

"I'm ancient. I'm allowed to watch whatever I want. And anyway, that's not even true. They've confiscated all sorts from me."

I opened my mouth to ask her what and then thought better of it.

"Shall we do your exercises now?" I asked her instead. The retirement home had told her she needed to improve her mobility, and I had offered to help her with stretches.

She nodded and heaved herself up off the bench.

"Good." It was an excuse to have a longer break before going back to sparring with Rory.

I raised my eyebrows in surprise when, instead of giving me shit or calling me lazy, Rory came to stand next to me. I stretched my arms out slowly to the side, giving Francis time to do the same. Rory copied us.

"Fancied joining in?" I asked her.

She shrugged. "Can't hurt."

My mind drifted as we bent and stretched and breathed deeply.

Maybe it hadn't been my mom. *Surely*, it hadn't been my mom.

Malc had made no progress on finding out who the

male voice belonged to. To be honest, we hadn't made much progress on anything. Envy was still hiding behind her social media profiles, Pride was lost in the ether, and we had found no leads at all on the book.

I was almost sure that Banks was the one behind the theft of the book. But even the might of the Ward hadn't been able to find him yet. Or poor Cheryl, the Warden he took with him as hostage when he escaped.

Heat suddenly washed over us on the breeze, and I whirled, forgetting Rory and Francis in a heartbeat. "Nox?"

I hadn't seen him in three days. And somehow, that was the longest we had been apart since he came into my life, offering me a deal I couldn't walk away from. A deal that led to the best night of my life.

He had been to visit Hell, to find out how the Hellhounds were escaping. He hadn't wanted to go, primarily because he wanted to avoid the god he hated so much, Examinus. But it was a lead only he could follow, and we were seriously short on other options.

Butterflies zoomed around in my stomach as his form grew larger against the blue sky as he got closer. How could a man I'd known for so little time have such an impact on both my mind and my body? When I hadn't been obsessing over my mom, I had been thinking about him non-stop, and I physically yearned for his touch so badly that I'd dreamed about it every night.

I moved away from Francis and Rory, and a few seconds later, Nox landed on the grass before me.

He was shirtless, golden wings breathtaking behind him, his dark hair wild. His eyes burned with blue fire as he took me in.

"Beth." He pulled me to him, and his skin was so hot I could barely stand it. But his lips met mine, and my own temperature soared to match.

"I missed you," I breathed against his mouth as his hungry kiss abated enough to speak.

"Good. I missed you too, though I would not have had you there with me." His eyes hardened with his words, and my face creased.

"What happened?"

"Examinus claims to know nothing of the Hell-hounds leaving Hell. He is lying to me. And he is not impressed with my progress on gathering back my power."

Nox's lip curled in anger and shadows swept across the light in his eyes. A little tingle of exhilaration bubbled up inside me and my brows rose in surprise at the response. *His shadows were exciting me?* That was new.

"Did you learn anything helpful?"

"No. He believes that my brothers are working for three other gods, and that they are behind both the thefts and the Hellhound escapes."

"And you don't?"

"No. Only a god or an angel with power rooted in Hell could free feral hounds from that realm."

"Are there many of those?"

"Two gods, including Examinus, and about a dozen angels - neither Michael nor Gabriel included. But Examinus would let me question none of them. He said it was an insult to even suggest it, when I should be gathering my strength, preparing to fight my true enemy." Nox made a snarling sound, and heat filled my chest.

"He really does sound like an asshole."

"Asshole doesn't come close." Nox tightened his grip around me and pulled me close to his chest. "I do not believe that you would like Hell much, Beth."

"No shit," I mumbled, leaning into his embrace and pressing my face to his hard, hot chest. "It's hardly tourist destination number one."

"At some point, soon, we will have to have the conversation we have been putting off." His voice was low, his chest rumbling against my cheek.

I blew out a sigh. I didn't want to think about Nox becoming the proper devil again, spending his days in Hell, punishing evildoers. Because I knew as well as he did that I couldn't live like that. I didn't even know if I could survive Hell - I was mortal.

But I knew why he was bringing it up. I could feel his heartbeat, racing in time with mine. I didn't think I was the only one who was starting to feel like a life where we were apart wasn't a life worth living.

TWO

BETH

"I'm going back to the office," said Rory loudly from behind us.

"It's evening," I said, turning to her. Nox's arm didn't loosen around me, barely giving me enough space to swivel.

She shrugged. "Got shit to do. See you both tomorrow." She nodded at Nox, then picked up her stuff from the bench.

Francis gave Nox a finger wave. "Hello, Mr. devil sir," she said. I felt his chest move as he chuckled.

"Hello, Francis," he called, and reached for my cheek, pulling me back around to face him. "I need to go home and sort a few things, and get the stench of Hell off me. Will you come to mine at eight?"

"Yes."

I'd be anywhere he told me to, whenever he told me to be there.

I lowered my voice. "I'm guessing, since you haven't gained any new power, we can't..."

His jaw tightened and he ground his teeth, then spoke. "If we were close to finding one of the lost sins, then we could risk it. But as it is..." He pushed his hand into my hair, gripping the back of my head. My breath hitched at his sudden intensity. "Beth, do not feel any guilt when I tell you this." His blue eyes burned, and I knew what he was going to say. "The weakening of my power became clear when I was in Hell."

Guilt did trickle through me, like icy poison dousing my elation at being with him again. "I'm sorry."

His grip tightened, and he kissed me. Not so hungrily, but just as intensely as before. "I'm not. I will never be sorry to bring you pleasure. I will never be sorry to claim you as my own. And I do not wish you to be."

He was telling the truth. His Lust power bared his intentions to me when we were this close, and I knew with every fibre of my being that he valued those blissful moments of passion with me more than his power. In fact, it wasn't just passion. His emotions radiated from him, seeping into me, penetrating all my barriers. He felt as deeply for me as I did for him.

"Nox..." He reached up, his fingers touching my lips, stilling my words before they came.

"I would like for us to continue this conversation later, when we are both more comfortable and somewhere more private." His trademark wicked smile took his lips. "I may want to say inappropriate things to you."

I bit my lip. "You know, Francis can't hear you from over there."

"All the same." He smiled. "I'll see you in a few hours."

After one last tender kiss he stepped backward. His wings snapped out behind him, and within a few great beats, he was rising through the air.

I watched him leave and made my way back over to Francis. "It sure is a shame you can't spend all day and all night riding that man like a damn race horse."

"I don't disagree," I told her.

"Have you ever done it while flying?" Her eyes lit up as she looked at me.

"No!"

"Why not? I would."

"I don't know if I would be able to concentrate." I waved my hands awkwardly. "Worse, I don't know if *he* would be able to concentrate. He might drop me."

"I'm sure he'd catch you."

She had a point; he probably would. The memory of him flying out of nowhere when I'd fallen from the tree, catching me in his arms like Superman, flashed into my head. Delicious heat ran through my body, concentrating at my core. Maybe Francis was onto something. "I'll think about it," I said. "But until we find his lost sins and get his power back, we can't do anything, flying or not. It weakens him. I will not be responsible for getting him killed." The firm words were as much a reminder to myself as Francis that sex with Nox was severely off limits.

She gave me a begrudging nod. "Yeah, I guess even great sex isn't worth dying for."

I blew out a sigh. Great sex didn't even come close to what it was like to be intimate with that man. *Angel*, I reminded myself. He wasn't a man. He was a fallen angel.

Part of me was reluctant to talk to him about the future. The other part of me couldn't believe he felt so strongly about me that the future was even a topic for discussion. Knowing my obsessive desire for him was mutual made my confidence soar. In fact, the warm, emboldening feeling I so often got when I was with him was starting to become a more constant companion, even when he wasn't around. I didn't know if it was the little ball of his power that now lived under my ribs, hot and fierce and a little scary, or if it was me.

I hoped it was me. It didn't feel alien, like his power did. It felt more like a sassier version of me was waking up. A version that wasn't scared of mom's scolding, or being left by men or friends for someone or something more exciting.

"Sun's going down," said Francis. "You gotta get ready for your date tonight."

"Could you hear us talking?" I asked her, surprised.

"Honey, I'm old, not deaf."

Slowly we walked across the gardens together, back to the retirement home. "Beth, do you think I'll ever be allowed to see Rory and all your magic stuff?"

"You saw the Hellhound."

"No, I saw the ground split and a whole bunch of crazy fiery shit."

"I could ask about lifting the Veil for you," I said. "But I've heard it's not easy."

Her face filled with excitement, and her pace increased a little. "You're sleeping with the devil, surely you have contacts?"

I smiled at her enthusiasm. "I'll ask Rory. She knows about this stuff."

Francis clapped her hands together. "Then I can join in with the self-defense classes!"

The idea of Francis sparring with the super-fit pixie made me laugh. "I can't wait to see Rory's reaction to that."

"I can't wait to just be able to *see* her," Francis answered.

"No promises, but I'll see what I can do."

"Ah shoot, I've left my water bottle out on the bench," said Francis, turning around.

"I'll get it," I told her, turning too.

"Thanks sweetie. Who's that?" Francis pointed. I saw a glimpse of a figure in a beige overcoat standing by the bench in the distance. They were too far away to make out, and I frowned.

"An orderly? Or a resident? Maybe they're getting your bottle. I'll go see."

I began a gentle jog toward the bench and the figure turned, heading toward the copse of trees. By the time I reached it, they were nowhere in sight. Francis' bottle was there though, so I picked it up and headed back to the retirement home.

"No idea who it was," I told Francis with a shrug. She had already installed herself in her Laz-y-boy.

"Never mind. You promise you'll ask about getting the Veil lifted for me?"

"I already said I would."

"No, you said *no promises*. I want a promise."

"I promise I'll ask. I can't do any more than that."

She gave me her brightest beam. "Thanks, Beth. You're an angel."

THREE

BETH

Claude was waiting outside my apartment when I left, and I happily followed him to where the town car was parked. When we got to Grosvenor Street, he pulled up outside Nox's ancient, gothic house, and the divider between the back of the car and the cab slowly moved down.

"Mr. Nox asked me to give you this," he said, and passed a small metal object through the window. I took it and couldn't help but smile.

A key.

"Thanks, Claude."

It felt weird, inserting the key into the enormous front door. It was not my home, nor anything like any home I would ever have expected to have a key for. But if Nox had asked for me to be given a key, I felt obliged to use it.

I pushed the front door open and heard Beelzebub

skittering across the wooden floors seconds before he came bounding down the hall. I laughed and said hello to him, inhaling the scent of coffee.

I followed the smell to the kitchen, where I found Nox leaning against the counter next to the coffee machine. He unfolded his arms, some of the tension leaving his body when he saw me.

My body, on the other hand, had tensed to the point of discomfort on seeing him.

He was wearing sweatpants, and a t-shirt so tight it was like skin. Every delicious curve of his muscles was on show, every ridge of his abs. He caught my too-slow perusal of him, and a wicked smile took his lips.

Heat pooled inside me, making me squeeze my thighs together.

"Good evening."

Good lord, that accent. I would never, ever tire of hearing him speak. "Hi," I said.

"How are you?"

"Good, thank you. You?"

"Much better for a shower and a workout. And the smell of coffee. You have mail." He nodded to an envelope on the counter next to a steaming espresso mug, and I frowned.

"Here?"

"I can't sense anything magical about it," he said, not hiding the suspicion in his voice. "But be careful. There's no address on it so it's not been sent through the mail. It's been put through the door by somebody."

I frowned as I sat on a stool and pulled the envelope

toward me. "Who would write to me here?" I started to say, but the words died on my lips.

"What's wrong?" Nox was at my side in an instant.

"It's been a long time, but... I could swear this is my mom's handwriting."

I stared down at my name, written in a pretty cursive, memories tumbling through my head.

Did Mom's writing look like that?

It couldn't be her writing. It simply couldn't.

Unable to contain my curiosity, I tore open the envelope. I felt Nox tense beside me, but when I tipped it cautiously upside down, all that fluttered out were two little pieces of paper. I reached for one of them.

"This is a Natural History Museum ticket."

Nox hissed out a breath. "One of the few places in the city I cannot go."

"Really?" I looked up surprised. "Why not?"

"A genie more powerful than Adstutus owns the Natural History Museum. And she doesn't like me much."

"Dare I ask why not?"

"Perhaps a story for another day," he said.

I swallowed my objection and turned the ticket over in my hands. Writing caught my attention. Writing in that same familiar scrawl. My stomach fluttered uneasily.

Ask about the Book of Sins.

· · ·

"Nox, look." He took the ticket, reading the words.

"And you think this is your Mom's writing?"

"How can it be?"

"Beth, I'm sorry to say this, but I think it is most likely someone trying to lure you into a trap." The sense in his words seeped through me, the glimmer of hope in my gut dying.

I looked at him. "The genie at this museum, could she have stolen your book?"

Nox grunted. "There's no way she would steal it, no. She is what you might call straitlaced. But I suppose someone might have tried to sell it to her."

"Someone like Max?"

"Someone exactly like Max." Nox's eyes sparked as he spoke.

"And would she have bought it from him? If she doesn't like you?"

"Perhaps. And then she'd have sold it on - not to the highest bidder, but to the person I would hate to have it the most."

"Who's that?"

He shrugged. "I've made a lot of enemies in my time."

"Would any of them taunt you with it? Hold it for ransom?"

"I imagine we'd have heard something by now. The book went missing weeks ago."

I reached for the cup of coffee and sipped. "Nox, I know you're not going to like this, but—"

He cut me off before I could finish the sentence. "You want to go to the museum."

I nodded. "We can't afford to not explore any leads." *Plus, that really, really did look like my Mom's handwriting.*

"I agree."

I raised my eyebrows, surprised. "Really? I thought you'd tell me it was too dangerous if you couldn't go with me." A little bubble of apprehension grew in my stomach. Had I wanted him to say it was too dangerous? I mean, if The Natural History Museum was one of the few places in the city Nox couldn't go, it was the perfect place for a trap. I felt a burn in my chest, and that new, but not unfamiliar, voice in my head piped up. *This is a chance to prove yourself. This is a chance to offer something to this situation that Nox can't. You can handle it. Remember how you handled Banks?*

The memory of Banks' nose crunching when I'd head-butted him made me sit straighter on my stool and hold Nox's look.

"We are not toys to be played with," he said, voice hard. "And we will not cower. Trap or not, whoever sent this knows something we don't."

I nodded. "We have to check it out. And Rory can go in the museum, right?"

"Yes. She will go with you. Technically, if it were a matter of life or death, I *could* enter the museum. But it would not be pretty, and the repercussions would be fierce."

If it came to it, then he could rescue me. Excitement

was pulsing through me, now. We had a lead, finally, and it was up to me to follow it.

Nox reached out, brushing his fingers along my jaw and drawing my face toward him. Shudders of pleasure pulsed out from his touch. He leaned over, touching his lips softly to mine.

"If anything happens to you..." His breath was warm against my mouth as he spoke between tender kisses. "I will burn this entire fucking world to the ground in retribution."

Excitement warred with horror at his words. Excitement that *he*, an all-powerful angel, could possibly feel so strongly about *me*, a boring mortal who likes romance books.

Horror because I believed him.

"The whole world? That seems a little excessive," I murmured against his lips.

"I have a temper."

I had seen Nox lose his temper, once high over the Thames with a prisoner in his grasp, and once helpless in magical cuffs and bound behind glass. He had been freaking fearsome both times.

"What's on the other piece of paper?" I asked, deciding to put a halt to that train of thought. And the kiss that was in danger of causing enough heat to build between my legs to melt my panties.

Nox leaned back with visible effort and picked up the other scrap of paper. He turned it to me, showing the symbol drawn on it. I recognized it instantly.

"That's it! That's the symbol I saw before!"

Nox frowned as he scrutinized it. "This is weirdly familiar. But I don't know why."

A tingling curiosity rippled through me. "I did a pretty bad sketch of this for Malc, but we should make sure he sees this version. It's much clearer."

Nox nodded. "I need to check in with him anyway."

Once the coffee had been replaced with a glass of delicious, deep red Malbec, Nox sat beside me and set up a video call on his laptop. Malc's pale face and red eyes appeared on the screen. "Boss," he nodded. "Lady Boss."

"Hi Malc," I said with a wave. "Any news on the recording?" I couldn't help asking.

"No, but I do have a lead on something else to do with your parents." My heart stuttered in my chest, and I leaned forward. "Adstutus sent us your blood test results, and I sent them on to a pal in South America, an alchemist, good with all chemicals." I willed him to get to the point faster. "She reckons she can work with the trace DNA."

"What do you mean *work with*?"

"She may be able to find out what kind of magic your parents had."

I felt a burst of hope. It wouldn't tell me where they were or if they were even alive, but it would tell me more about them than what I currently knew. "How long will that take him?"

"I have a call with her tomorrow. I'll let you know what she says right away."

"Malc, thank you. Thank you so much."

The vampire shrugged. "Just doing my job, Lady Boss."

"Well, I appreciate it. Although I'm not sure how I feel about Lady Boss."

"You'll get used to it." His red eyes flashed with amusement.

"I quite like it," said Nox, and I punched him in the arm. He ignored me and held the piece of paper with the symbol on it up to the camera. "Beth had this delivered today. It's a more accurate version of what she saw on Banks."

"Okay, photograph it and send it to me for now, but make sure you bring me the actual parchment ASAP—there might be clues on it."

"I'll deliver it myself tomorrow. Is Rory there?"

Rory appeared on the screen a few minutes later. "Rory, I need you to spend the day with Beth tomorrow." The pixie's face didn't change, cool as always.

"Fine. Call me when you need me." Rory disappeared off camera and Malc pulled a face at me.

"I'm sure you two will get along like a house on fire in no time at all," he grinned.

I gave him a sarcastic smile back. "No doubt." Although I was starting to suspect that the angry pixie liked me better now than when she first met me. And I was positive that she could help me get closer to being able to protect myself. The problem was, everybody had magic except me.

"Nox, is there anything I can use to defend myself against magic? In place of having any of my own?"

He looked at me thoughtfully for a moment, then at Malc. "I know a couple of weapons that can be wielded by mortals."

"I'll get on it," Malc said.

"Good. See you tomorrow."

When the laptop was closed, Nox looked at me. "I'm trying very, very hard not to scoop you up off that stool, take you upstairs, and learn what makes you scream my name the loudest, Miss Abbott."

I squirmed on my seat, my cheeks and core heating. "You know it's not fair to talk like that. We can't do anything."

"Then distract me. Before I lose control."

"Here's an idea," I said, refusing to let my gaze move from his face, lest it devour that delicious body. "We don't talk about Hell or sins or angels or parents - any of it. We just talk. To each other. About each other."

His dirty smile slowly changed into something more sincere. "I think that's a fucking fantastic idea."

My heart swelled in my chest. "Can we play cribbage too?"

"You can't be serious. Your favorite film is Top Gun?"

Nox shrugged as he stared down at the cards fanned out in his hand. "You can't beat that soundtrack."

"I couldn't agree more."

He looked up at me, light shining in his eyes. "Really?"

"Absolutely."

"Which song is your favorite?"

I couldn't help smirking as I looked down at my own cards. I had an amazing hand. "I'll tell you, if you beat me."

His gaze danced over my face, then he nodded. We scored our hands, and as I had known I would, I beat him.

"So. You have to tell me your favorite song. No wait - let me guess."

He leaned back on the sofa.

"It's Dangerzone, isn't it." I said, triumphantly.

Slowly, he shook his head, then stood up, making his way over to a hifi in the corner of the room that looked older than me. He pressed a few buttons, and the opening beats of Take My Breath Away filled the room.

"The devil is into power ballads?" I smiled at him as he turned back to me.

"Yup. The more eighties, the better." His eyes darkened, and he held out his hand. "Dance with me?"

Wild horses couldn't stop me.

I leaped up, taking his warm palm. He pulled me tight against his chest, and I wrapped my arms around his muscular back, breathing in his presence. Together we swayed to the music.

"I told you I was better at crib than poker," I mumbled into his shirt.

"It's been a while since I played. I'm rusty."

"Excuses, excuses."

He dipped his head, and I brought mine up to meet him. His kiss told me he was trying to keep things light, playful.

The song changed, and the sound of Kenny Loggins burst into the room, guitar and eighties cheese galore.

I laughed, and Nox eyes shone as he lifted my hand, spinning me around.

"You're intoxicating."

"You're not bad yourself," I grinned at him, between spins.

He caught me tight in his hold, ducking so his lips were a mere inch from mine.

"I'm serious, Beth. You're like a drug. Something I can't get enough of, or ever imagine being without."

My pulse raced as he spoke, his scent, his power, his words all coming together to make my stomach flip.

"I'm not going anywhere."

"Say it."

I knew what he wanted to hear. His Lust power made the word echo through my mind.

"Yours."

"Mine."

Images of him claiming me, mind, body and soul, naked and hot in tangled sheets, bare skin and rippling muscles flooded my head, and I gasped aloud.

He abruptly pulled his arms from me as though he'd

been stung, stepping backward. Hunger burned so hot in his gaze that he looked almost feral.

"I must go. Now."

More images crashed through my mind. Me moaning his name as he filled me, me sat in his lap rocking hard-

"Now. Goodnight, Beth."

With a last, scorching look, he swept from the room.

I stared after him, the ache between my legs becoming painful.

The old me, the pre-Nox me, would have been worried that he was rejecting me. That he didn't want me.

But this Beth knew he was leaving exactly because of how much he did want me. He didn't trust himself to keep control.

And it wasn't just Lust we were struggling to control any more. There was so much emotion flowing between us. Not just any old emotion either. I was increasingly suspicious that it was love.

Just thinking about him made a feeling expand through my whole body, a sense of everything being okay, of the world being right. Fierce desire that bordered on possessiveness filled me when I thought about all the things that could keep us apart.

And until we dealt with them, we couldn't be together. Nox had to get the book, the sins, and his power back.

FOUR

Nox leapt up from a stool as soon as I entered the kitchen the next morning. "I'm sorry. About last night. I-"

"You don't need to explain," I said, cutting him off. "I can see your desires, remember?" I smiled at him and saw relief in his bright eyes.

He kissed me, softly. "You look nice."

"Really? Thanks." I was wearing jeans and a satin shirt. Nox looked a lot smarter, as usual, in expensive slacks and a pale blue shirt.

"Coffee?"

I slid onto what had become my stool—in my mind at least—and watched him move around the beautiful kitchen.

"You know, I could get used to this view," I told him.

"That's the goal."

Nervous excitement fluttered in my gut.

"Do you still want to go to the museum this morning?"

The nervous excitement fluttered harder. It was my turn to show up, to offer something to the plan. "Damn straight."

~

"So, why doesn't this genie we're going to see like you?"

Mischief swirled in Nox's eyes as he looked at me in the back of Claude's car. "She's called Techa. And I stole her statue."

"Her statue?"

"Yes. A bust of Aphrodite. Very valuable and very powerful."

Rory was sitting to Nox's left, staring straight out of the window. I got the distinct impression she was pretending she was somewhere else.

"Why did you steal it?"

Nox grinned at me. "It has the power to incite overly-affectionate behavior in humans."

I raised my eyebrows. "Go on."

"I took it on tour. For most of the 1960s."

I shook my head. "The swinging sixties. So Malc wasn't exaggerating when he said you misbehaved for decades."

Nox flashed me a wicked smile. "Harmless fun."

Sex with Nox was sure as hell more than harmless fun. It was life-alteringly fantastic fun. Devastatingly addictive fun. Mind-blowingly—

"Here we are." Rory announced, interrupting my spiraling sex-adjective thoughts.

I peered through the window and saw the beautiful exterior of the Natural History Museum growing larger as we approached. Built from alternating orange and grey bricks, it looked more like a cathedral at first glance. The shape was distinctly church-like at the front, with two tall square spires heralding the entrance. I had seen the museum from the outside before and noted the pretty brick colors, but I had never been inside.

I turned to Nox and was alarmed to see how tight his expression was. "Are you okay?"

"I can't go any further. Not comfortably. Will you be alright to walk from here?"

"Yes, of course."

Claude pulled the car over to the side of the road, and I opened the door. "Please, be careful. Call me immediately if you need any help." The playfulness had gone completely from Nox's face.

"I will. Where are you going?"

"Not far."

I nodded. "See you soon."

Rory and I walked up the grand steps together, and I wondered how we would find the woman we were looking for. "Rory, do you know anything about this genie?"

"Not much. But I know how to get to the magic part of the museum. We'll start there."

I gazed up at the beautiful archway above us as we reached the main entrance, shaking my head. "I can't believe I never knew magic existed my whole life. The museum has *magic parts?*"

We had reached the ticket booth just inside the entrance, and Rory looked expectantly at me. I stepped forward and asked for two tickets, dropping a five-pound note into the donation box, before moving into the main hall.

My breath caught as I looked around. An enormous chamber with beautiful, vaulted ceilings housed a mezzanine floor framed with impossibly grand arches and columns, and all of it was built from the same orange and grey brick as the exterior. Smack-bang in the center of the epic space the was the mammoth skeleton of a dinosaur. I stared up at it as I walked under its long neck.

"Is this magic?" I half-whispered. The thought of the dinosaur bones coming to life was both thrilling and terrifying at once.

"No." Rory barely looked at the ginormous skeleton as she walked. I was disappointed that we weren't heading up the grand central staircase at the opposite end, instead turning down a corridor filled with stuffed replicas of extinct creatures. A large bear that looked a lot like it should live in the arctic loomed up on its back legs behind the glass, a tiny white fox with beady eyes sat at its feet.

"What about these?"

Rory sighed. "None of the objects out here are magical."

"Out here?"

She waved her hand vaguely. "On public display."

"Oh."

We reached the end of the animals corridor and she headed through some doors. The kid in me wanted to clap my hands together as I entered the room. It was *full* of dinosaurs. A walkway rose above us, allowing visitors to see the tops of the massive replicas of the ancient beasts more easily, but we stayed on the ground, weaving between display cases of bones and fossils. I itched to stop and read the information boards, but Rory kept a brisk pace, and I daren't slow her down. She was clearly a woman on a mission.

Soon, we entered a room that was darker than the others, lit with eerie blue and orange spotlights that sent shadows in every direction. Dominating the room was a life-size Tyrannosaurus Rex, standing in a set designed to look like its natural habitat. I couldn't help my grin as it moved, making a young woman cry out in surprise ahead of us. A roaring sound came from speakers that must have been hidden in the walls, and the girl laughed as she clutched her partner's arm.

A museum was a great place for a date, I thought wistfully. Shame Nox couldn't come here. Thinking of his serious face when he'd warned me to be careful made my smile slip away. *Focus, Beth. This is serious.*

The animatronic dinosaur swung its head toward us, and Rory stopped in front of it, making a *tsking* sound. More roaring filled the room.

With another shake of her head, she climbed over the

safety rail. Not an easy feat, given that she was wearing a shin length pencil-skirt, but she made it look effortless.

Although I knew perfectly well that the creature was a robot, instinct made my stomach twist as she neared it. It was *not* about to bite her head off, but a surge of protective instinct took me, and I hurried over the barrier to catch her up.

The dinosaur's head swung low, its big fake teeth making me swerve back, despite the lack of real threat.

"I'm sure it's here," Rory said from where she was standing, directly under the dinosaur's belly. She stamped her foot on the floor, and a shimmering blue rippled out from the contact. The roaring of the dinosaur seemed tinny and far away for a second and then a staircase appeared in the wall behind the creature's tail. It was as grand as all the others in the place, old, polished stone and finely made bricks, and it was so seamlessly a part of the building that I couldn't believe it hadn't been there a second ago.

Rory turned and headed toward it. I snapped my mouth shut and followed her.

The corridor at the top of the stairs felt like part of a gallery. Alcoves in the walls, which had the same beautiful sweeping arch shapes as the main hall, held a vast array of objects, and I was happy that Rory wasn't moving as fast as she had through the dinosaurs. It meant I had enough time to peer at each thing as we passed. There were fossils belonging to creatures I wouldn't have been able to even picture, if it weren't for the sketches displayed beside them. There were creatures that looked vaguely like trolls, three headed-lions, enormous centaurs, minuscule lizards - all sorts.

"Are all these extinct from the magical world now?" I asked Rory. She was glancing at the alcoves as we walked too.

"Sadly, yes."

I looked at a bone larger than me, the sketch beside it depicting what could have been a dragon - except that its fanged mouth took up ninety percent of its head. It was a shame it was extinct, but I sure as hell wouldn't want to run into one. Much like a T-rex, I supposed.

There were no tourists or visitors in the corridor, and it was oddly quiet compared to the part of the museum we had just come from. "Where do we find the genie?" I asked.

"I don't know."

We kept moving until we reached the end of the corridor. Hallways led off to the left and right, but I couldn't tear my eyes from the painting on the wall to look down either of them.

It was so large that, if it was laid flat on the ground, it would probably have covered the entire floor of my living room in my apartment.

It showed a world beyond the limit of my imagination. On the right of the panel was a clifftop, with an army of creatures crowded across it. Everything I had ever seen in a movie, in these corridor halls, and more, were depicted. Above all the land creatures, filling a bright blue sky, was a myriad of flying beasts, including the owner of the bone I had just seen. Eagles as big as planes, ridden by weapon-wielding figures swooped over the cliffs.

On the left of the panel was the ocean, also filled with beasts that looked as prehistoric and mean as anything in the museum. But the blue of the ocean melted into a fiery orange world below it. Demons, horned and naked, were dragging down fish and shark alike, and all the creatures with limbs were trying to claw their way up the cliff.

Above the ocean, and the escaping demons, were three figures, hovering in the sky. Two had white wings and halos. But the one in the center, dark and fearsome, had burning golden wings.

Nox.

Only... He wasn't Nox here. He was Lucifer. Punisher of Sinners. Lord of Evil.

I felt the hair on my skin rise as I stepped closer, my fingers reaching out of their own volition to touch the image of the man I was falling in love with.

But he was no man. He was an angel. A deity in his own right. The painting was a stark reminder of who he was, so vivid in its simplicity. It didn't show him as evil. Not like paintings of the devil I had seen growing up. It showed him for what he truly was. Part of a trio of powerful beings, needed to keep the world in balance.

He had neglected his duties for only a blink of an eye, in his terms. But everything had begun to crumble around him. His brothers' words came back to me, their pleas for him to retake his role. With a crushing, finite clarity, I knew that Nox would never be free from what he was born to do. It was his fate, His destiny. His purpose.

"Are you ready?" Rory's voice was soft, but it startled me all the same.

"He's not evil," I said, turning to her, feeling a little dazed.

"He is not good either. Beth, an absence of cruelty and an abundance of passion does not make a person good."

"That depends on your definition."

Her gaze bore into mine. "Yes. You might be right, there."

"I am. I know I am." I had to be. Because I couldn't love a man with no good in his heart. That wasn't me.

I blew out a sigh as Rory moved down the left corridor, then looked at the painting one last time. Even in painted form, Nox's golden wings made my breath catch.

He was the devil. An almighty, fearsome angel. And somehow, more important to me than should even be possible.

FIVE

The corridor we were walking down held no alcoves, but more paintings. Some were of creatures, but most were landscapes. I recognized many as typically European or Asian, but none as a specific location. We passed a few closed doors but stopped at none.

Soon, the images on the walls changed to representations of gemstones, and I saw that the end of the corridor was a decorative set of doors into another room. "The gem room," Rory muttered as we walked through them.

It was like being at the world's most expensive jewelry store. Glass-topped counter after counter ran the length of the vaulted room, and I stared down into them, mouth agape. Each display held a different type of stone, and although they all looked like the ones in the human world, there was something subtly different about each.

"You smell like the devil."

The crisp female voice rang through the room, and

Rory and I both froze. An unsettling cold crept over me, and the silence of the space became oppressive.

"Hello!" I said to the room at large, forcing a polite cheeriness into my voice. "I might smell a bit like him, yes. We're, erm, friends."

"Then you are not welcome." The slight chill turned to ice. My feet began to tingle unpleasantly.

"I just had a question for you, as we're here. We are trying to find the Book of Sins, and have reason to believe someone may have tried to sell it to you recently." I flexed my fingers, trying to dispel the cold from them.

"The Book of Sins?" The voice changed from aloof to interest. With a shimmer, similar to the one that preceded Adstutus' appearances, a woman materialized in front of us. She was gorgeous. Like, ridiculously beautiful. Tomb Raider meets librarian, was my first thought, as I took in her long, thick braid, black-rimmed glasses, and full mouth. She was wearing a pantsuit and had piercingly violet eyes. "Why do you want the Book of Sins? Do you intend to return it to its rightful owner?"

"Erm..." I blew on my hands as I tried to work out what to tell her and shifted from foot to foot to try to stop my toes from losing all feeling. "Yes," I said, opting to be truthful.

The beautiful genie raised one perfect eyebrow. "Please leave."

The temperature dropped again, and my breath caught in shock at the cold. "Would it change your mind if I told you that he wants to retake his proper place?"

The violet eyes pinned me where I was, and I

stopped rubbing my hands together. "His proper place? Please expand."

"As the punisher. He wants all seven sins back, so that he can regain his full power and retake his role in Hell." I was hoping that the genie shared a mindset with Nox's brothers and believed that the best place for Nox was punishing sinners in Hell, where he belonged.

The genie's eyes narrowed as she tilted her head at me. "You are not a sinner. Or an angel."

I shook my head. "No. I'm mortal. And I think I'm morally virtuous. Sort of. At least, I'm not an asshole." I forced myself to close my chattering lips and hold my babbling in, as the genie lifted a finger to her mouth, running her manicured nail along her lip thoughtfully.

"I will set you a test. If you pass it, then I will tell you what I know about the books whereabouts."

"Do you know where it is?"

She nodded slowly, her braid moving. "Yes. It has recently crossed my path."

Excitement thrilled through me, expelling some of the cold. "What kind of test?"

"A test of character. If I deem you worthy, then I shall give you what you require."

"That sounds fair."

The genie gestured to the closest cabinet, the glass covered in an icy frost. "Choose one."

"Huh?"

"You are deaf? Or stupid?"

I bristled, and glared at her. "No. I am... confused," I finished lamely. With a huff, I stepped toward the cabinet. The covering of ice vanished so that I could see clearly.

There were three gems inside. One was red and orange, with jagged edges and flecks of black. The middle one was a clear purple, and I was almost sure I could see waves inside it. The last was the shape of an egg and deep black, flecked with glittering gold. It reminded me instantly of Nox.

Was this part of the test? Should I choose the one least like Nox? Or should I choose the one I was genuinely drawn to?

"That one." I pointed to the black and gold egg.

The beautiful genie gave me a suspicious, knowing look, and the cabinet clicked open. She gave a little flick of her hand, and the egg floated up and out of the case toward me.

I opened my hand, still shaking with the cold, and let it float down into my palm.

Electricity tore through my body. I cried out, but instead of dropping the egg, my fingers curled around it, clutching it tighter. The pain abruptly stopped.

"What is happening?" The stone moved, and it was getting hot. "Why is it moving?" I looked up at the genie. Her expression had changed, becoming one of genuine interest.

"You won't be able to hide those anymore," she mused, eyes flicking over my shoulders. I realized dimly that she must be talking about my wings. "That stone was the right choice for you. Any other, and you would have remained powerless."

"What? What are you talking about?" The egg wiggled again, and I thought I heard a noise.

"That stone is from Hell. All three stones contain a companion of mine who can watch you over the next few days and determine your worthiness." I opened my mouth but she kept talking. "That stone has had the added side effect of amplifying the power that is already inside you. It will stop when you return the stone to me."

The heat coming from the stone in my hand clashed with my numb fingers and freezing skin, and adrenaline built inside me, fueled by anxiety.

"You have the magic of the devil in you. I do not know how it came to be this way, or what will happen if Lucifer really does decide to take back all of his power, but for now, it is there, burning inside your body."

I stared at her, blinking through confusion. "I can't do anything with that power, or these wings. It's just... there."

"You are far more interesting than I originally assumed. This is Behemoth. He will report back to me on your integrity when your time is up. Farewell."

With another shimmer, the genie was gone, and I found myself staring at a goat.

A miniature pygmy goat. Standing in the middle of the gem room. He was jet black, and just like the egg stone, he had gold flecks all over his fur that caught the bright lights in the room. Huge gold horns curled up out of his head, and his black eyes lacked the vacant stupidity most goats I'd seen possessed.

"B-behemoth?" I whispered.

"Yup." The voice was in my head and frightened the shit out of me. Rory must have heard it too, because she gave a small hiss. I took a deep breath.

"You're a goat."

"A Hell-goat," he corrected me.

"What is a Hell-goat?"

"Same as a normal goat, except I got some upgrades." He trotted around in a circle, as though showing off his upgrades, and stopped in front of me. "So, I'm your new companion, huh?"

"Erm..." I trailed off. "Were you inside that stone?"

"Yes. It is my home. But I am frequently entrusted with important missions outside of the stone." I saw a flash of gold in his eyes as he spoke, and there was a twinge of excitement in his tone.

"So, erm, you're going to judge my integrity?" I felt like I needed to sit down. The icy cold was seeping from the room though, and the egg stone had stopped radiating heat.

"You appear to be a bit slow." He sounded worried. "Yes. I will be your temporary companion, to determine if you have a righteous soul and are worth my master's time and help. I thought she made that pretty clear."

I stared down at the goat. "I'm sorry, I just... I never met a Hell-goat before."

"Well, I am quite magnificent. I can see why you might get flustered in my presence."

"You look quite... *small* for a Hell-goat named Behemoth. And kind of cute," said Rory, coming to stand next to me. Her lips had a tinge of blue to them, and like me, she had goosebumps over her bare arms.

She was right, Behemoth was quite cute. He stamped his little hooves on the ground, and the gold flashed in his eyes again.

"I assure you, I am not cute. I am a menacing Hellbeast."

"Right."

"Pray you never see me when I'm angry."

I couldn't help the corners of my mouth twitching up in a smile as the fluffy little goat lifted his chin, the haughty words ringing inside my skull. "I don't want to see you angry," I assured him.

"Good. Now, can we go? I've been in this museum for months, and I'm hungry."

By the time we reached the dinosaur exhibit, I had finally stopped shivering. Behemoth trotted along by my side, tutting and muttering at the replica prehistoric beasts. Snatches of his words floated through my head, mostly stuff about humans not knowing the half of what a real monster looked like.

"The boss isn't going to like this," said Rory, glancing down at the goat. "He's basically a spy for one of his most powerful enemies in London."

"I don't think we've got much choice. And besides, I'm a good person. So Behemoth will discover that and tell Techa and then she'll tell us where the book is. I'd say this was a resounding success."

Even if I did now have a Hell-goat companion. And a very weird sense of many humans around me being assholes.

I needed to talk to Nox about his power as soon as I saw him, I thought, as a prickling, uncomfortable feeling washed over me as we passed close to a man leering at a pretty museum guide. Was I sensing the sin of Lust in the man?

The prickling feeling was abruptly washed away as a wave of sensation crashed over me, making my steps falter. Anger, hot and fierce and righteous inexplicably filled my chest, making both my fists and jaw clench.

"Beth. How nice to see you," a sharp but silky voice called out. My gaze fell on Madaleine as she strode across the museum hall toward us. Somehow, she managed to make the enormous skeleton beside her seem smaller in her presence. She looked immaculate, as usual, and was dressed in white. Cornu sauntered along a step behind her, wearing his permanently filthy smile.

I forced myself to relax, to not let her power overwhelm me. I felt the heat in my chest that I knew was Nox's power flare to life, and a calming warmth flooded my body. Was this what Nox felt all the time? An ability to just zone out others with his weird warmth blanket?

I schooled my face into indifference as the angel of Wrath stopped before me, not wanting her to know I was experiencing anything out of the ordinary. She looked straight down at Behemoth, then at my wings. Her eyes narrowed.

"You and Nox are getting close, if he's giving you Hell pets." She stroked Cornu's arm. "I am a fan myself, of course."

"He's just a temporary thing," I said awkwardly.

She raised one eyebrow. "Nox, or the goat?"

"The goat."

"Well, don't forget, sweetie, that *you* are just a temporary thing to the Lord of Hell. Your lifespan is a mere blip on his."

Anger surged in me. I knew what she'd said was true, but I didn't want to think about it. "Right. Thanks for that reminder. We'll be going now. I don't want to keep you from..." I stopped speaking, adopting the same suspicious look she'd worn when she'd seen Behemoth. "What *are* you doing here?"

"Just a little sightseeing," she shrugged.

"Bullshit." I folded my arms across my chest, and her smile morphed from sarcastic to something more sincere.

"You know, he's rubbing off on you." She looked pointedly at my wings again. "Quite literally, it would seem."

"What do you want, Madaleine?"

"I want more than your mortal brain can even comprehend," she said, with a small sigh. I was almost sure her gaze flicked to Cornu for a split second. "But right now, I want you to know that I am not your enemy. I respect Lucifer. I don't respect *you* yet, but I feel like I could. Maybe."

I said nothing, but the heat inside me roiled. The weird thing was, *I* wanted to like *her*. Annoying as I found it, I admired her. Her presence, her power, her indomitable aura, it was all unavoidably impressive to me.

"If you want to improve your poker skills, let me know," she continued. "And I meant what I said about mortal lifespans. If you're serious about him, and he you, you're going to have to fix that." The anger swelled again, as though even talking about the possibility of Nox and I not being together sparked it to life.

"What would you know about long-term relationships?" I kept my arms folded and gestured my head at Cornu. "You employ pets for company."

This time I definitely saw something in her eyes, and in the twitch of her beautiful face. Was it annoyance with me, or something to do with Cornu? Either way, I'd hit a nerve.

"Yes. I do," she said, her cool tone belying the flash of emotion. "For good reason. Would you like to know what happens when a mortal lover fails to satisfy a fallen angel with the power of Wrath?"

I swallowed. Nope. I didn't want to know. Madaleine tipped her head slightly, in a didn't-think-so kind of way. "Well, if you feel like being more friendly, Lucifer has my number." With a flick of her hand, she strode on past us before I could think of anything to say.

"I don't trust her," said Rory quietly.

"I quite liked her," Behemoth's voice said in my head. "Can I have a burger?"

"A burger?"

"I love burgers."

I needed the little goat to like me, and if the easiest way to make that happen was feed him burgers, then that's what I would do. "Yes, of course you can. We'll go to Solum, and you can have whatever you want," I said, resuming walking to the exit.

"Excellent. I haven't been to Solum in a while. Is Adstutus still there?"

I raised my eyebrows. "You know him?"

I didn't hear the goats answer though, because something caught my eye. The flash of a beige overcoat. I paused, trying to focus, but there were a lot of people in the huge hall and columns and exhibits everywhere blocked my view.

Madaleine disappeared into the dinosaur exhibit, closely followed by someone in a beige overcoat, their hood up.

"What's wrong?" Rory's voice snapped me out of my staring.

"I-I thought I saw something."

"What?"

"Someone in a beige overcoat, following Madaleine."

Rory gave me her trademark 'are-you-stupid?' look. "Right. You know there are literally hundreds of tourists in here, all going to the dinosaur exhibit. Many wearing coats."

"Yeah, but I thought I saw someone yesterday in the same one."

Rory shook her head. "Do you want to go back? I'm not sure Techa will be pleased. And Nox is waiting."

"No. I'm sure it's nothing. Let's leave."

We resumed heading toward the exit, and when we reached the massive door I found myself relieved to be outside. My cell phone rang as soon as I started down the steps. The screen told me it was Nox.

"You have a Hell-creature with you." His voice was granite.

"Yeah. Behemoth. Apparently, he's a Hell-goat. A miniature one."

"Fucking goats," Nox sighed, his tone relaxing. "Why do you have a Hell-goat with you?"

"It's probably easier to explain in person. And I just promised him a burger. Where are you?"

"I'll pick you up."

SIX

BETH

"So? Is Adstutus still in Solum?" Behemoth asked me. I glanced down at him as we made our way down the steps, heading back to the part of the sidewalk where Nox had dropped us off.

"Yeah, he is. He made me the potion that was hiding my wings."

"Why, exactly, were you hiding them? You should be proud of them. They mark you as part of Hell. They're clearly not as magnificent as I am, but still. You shouldn't hide them."

"Nox thought it would be best if others didn't know."

I wasn't sure how wise it was to be honest with the miniature goat, but if he was going to be observing me, there seemed little point lying to him.

And besides, if what the genie had said was true, I wouldn't be able to hide the wings now, anyway, and they were clearly little versions of Nox's. A ripple of excitement made its way through my body at the thought.

Even before getting the black and gold egg, I'd been feeling Nox's power inside me, stronger and stronger each time I was tested. There had been moments when I had been with Banks, at the Ward HQ, that I'd really believed it was giving me a tangible confidence - or maybe anger - that had helped me.

If I was being totally honest with myself, I was actually starting to hope that I *would* be able to access, or even better use, the power.

"I have never met Lucifer. Nox, as you call him." Behemoth bounced a little as he pranced along, making him look even cuter.

"I'm sure you'll like him." I wasn't so sure the feeling would be mutual though.

We didn't have to wait by the side of the road, as the town car was already there. Nox was leaning against it, his expression tense. I didn't know if that was due to his proximity to the building or my new companion.

"If you don't need me anymore, I'll go back the office," said Rory.

Nox nodded at her and she started to turn, but I caught her arm.

"Thanks," I said.

She shrugged her elegant shoulders. "I didn't do anything."

"All the same. Thanks." She held my eye contact for a promising moment, and I decided to seize the opportunity. "Also, before I forget... Could you do me a favor?" She raised one perfect eyebrow. "Do you think you could get the Veil lifted for Francis?"

To my surprise, she gave a small laugh, then seemed to catch herself, expression turning serious again. "That woman would lose her shit if she could see magic."

"I know. It could be quite fun. And she's desperate to see you."

For the first time ever, I saw something soften in the pixie's eyes. "I'll see what I can do," she said, whirled on her heels, and clicked away.

Nox said nothing as we got into the car, me lifting Behemoth up when he failed to jump quite high enough to reach the seat.

When the vehicle set off, he stared at the little black-and-gold goat.

"See," said Behemoth, turning to me, then looking back at Nox. "That's what Hell looks like on an angel. Truly magnificent."

Nox raised one eyebrow, so I assumed he could hear him, too.

"Nox looks human right now," I said. "He doesn't have his wings out, or anything that looks hell-like going on with his appearance."

"Not to me."

"Oh."

"Beth, please update me on what the fuck is going on." Nox's hard eyes flashed as they found mine.

I took a breath. "Techa says that she knows where the book is, and she'll tell me if she deems me worthy. And she is going to test my worthiness by having Behemoth here watch me for a while and report back to her."

Shadows swirled through Nox's bright eyes. "And there's more," I said.

"I can see that." His eyes flicked over my shoulders, and I guessed he could see my wings too.

"She gave me this stone, which apparently is Behemoth's home, and said it unlocked my powers because it's from Hell?" I fished the stone out of my pocket.

Nox gazed down at the stone but made no move to take it. "She gave you that?"

"Sort of. I had to choose between three."

His eyes snapped to mine. "And you chose that one? Why?"

"It... It reminded me of you."

Heat pulsed from him, wrapping around me, and the shadows were chased away from his irises by a burst of blue light. His gaze held mine for a moment that was both too long and too short, all at the same time. Then he spoke.

"Let's get some coffee, and I'll tell you what I can."

Nox was silent the entire way to Solum. He said nothing as we made our way through the bookshop and found the special book that revealed the secret marketplace underneath Covent Garden. And he said nothing as we walked through the packed stalls, scores of magical creatures milling around us, almost all of them stealing glances at both him and the little black and gold goat at my feet.

Possibly they were looking at me too, I thought, conscious of my wings in a way I hadn't been before.

Unlike Nox, Behemoth had plenty to say. In fact, he didn't really stop talking.

Question after question came from the little goat, both about me in general, and about the current state of the world. After telling him where I lived, that I was in fact human and that I had only discovered magic very recently and therefore couldn't answer anything about magical politics, he moved on to telling me about himself.

Apparently, he was from a big family, but was one of only three miniature Hell-goats - the rest of his sixty-three siblings were full size. Rather than have a chip on his shoulder about his diminished stature though, he seemed quite proud.

"The thing about being rare," he said as he trotted along, "is that you have something that others don't."

"But what if that's not a good thing?" I said hesitantly, not wanting to offend the creature when we needed him on-side.

He looked up at me, gold horns gleaming and his onyx eyes weirdly expressive. "What do you mean?"

"Like, what if the thing about you that is different is a bad thing?"

He snorted, an actual farm-animal sound. "No such thing. If you've got it, and others don't, revel in it."

"You sure have a lot of confidence crammed into that furry little body."

"It's not confidence," he told me. "It's certainty in my

own ability. I am mighty. And beautiful too." I smiled down at him. I was finding it impossible not to like him.

"There's a truth in his words," Nox said quietly from my other side. I had assumed he'd stopped listening to the goat's incessant chatter long ago.

"You think he's beautiful too?" I grinned at Nox.

He gave me a look. "There's a place where confidence crosses into certainty. You will find this place. I will make sure of it."

"Hmmm. Then will I have an ego the size of Behemoth's?"

"I think you would be surprised how good an ego would look on you, Miss Abbott."

The coffee shop was busy when we arrived, but that didn't stop the waiter finding a table in the middle of the room to settle us at. Behemoth insisted on sitting on his own upholstered chair on the other side of Nox. To his credit, the waiter didn't even blink at the goat's demands as he took our order.

"The magic that keeps Behemoth tethered to that stone is ancient, and powerful," Nox said, once our coffees had been brought over. "It is the same magic that tethers genies to their hosts. But the stone itself has its own power, separate from that."

Behemoth nodded his head, his gold horns moving. "The stone is from Mount Ignis."

Nox raised an eyebrow at him. "How do you know that?"

"It's my home," the goat snorted.

"It imparts information?"

"Yes. It has a soul."

"The stone has a soul?" I echoed.

Nox looked at me. "Sort of. Not in the way that you or I, or even Behemoth here, has. But it has a living energy. Hell is not a place like this world. It is made up entirely of what you would call magic, and its lifeblood is living energy drawn from the souls who inhabit it. That stone is part of Hell itself, and so, it is made up of that energy."

"The stone has part of the souls of people who live in Hell inside it?" The thought made me uneasy. "Don't sinners and evil people live in Hell?"

Nox nodded. "Yes."

"And... I was drawn to it?"

"Yes."

I let out a long breath. "How has that made my wings show?"

"That same energy is what you have drawn from me. The stone is amplifying it. It recognizes you as its own."

Unable to work out how I felt about that without a long bath and a glass of wine, I moved on to my most pressing question.

"There's something else." I cast my eyes to Behemoth, who stared back at me, unblinking. There was no point hiding anything from him, I decided. I was a good person, and I would be myself and be honest in his presence. "I can feel your power. Like actually doing something. I'm sure I felt Lust from a guy in the museum - not toward me-" I added quickly as Nox's face turned stormy. "And when I saw Madaleine and her power made me angry, that warmth thing you do to me happened, but from inside me."

Nox tilted his head and wetted his lips with his tongue. Desire pulsed, unbidden, through my whole body. "Madaleine was there?"

"Yes. But tell me about the power."

His piercing blue gaze bore into mine. "I'm sorry, Beth, but I can't tell you much. I have never, ever been in this situation before. I have passed the sin powers to others via the book, which is an extraordinarily powerful artifact, but this is different. The power you have drawn from me is my own, and the magic used to curse me is godly and beyond my understanding. This is as new to me as it is to you."

I stared back at him. "Do you think I can use the power? Now I have the stone?"

"It sounds like the magic is responding to you and the things around you."

"I think it is protecting me. And sometimes... Some-times making me bolder."

Nox nodded his head a tiny bit, and I thought he looked relieved. "I don't know if you will actually be able to control it, but it might help you with whatever is coming our way."

"Okay. Good. I think."

"What did Madaleine want?" The intensity left his expression and he picked up his coffee.

"I don't know why she was in the museum, but she told me she wanted to play poker with me."

"We should worry if she is visiting Techa. If she's after the book, too..." He looked thoughtful as he drank.

"But she tipped us off about Sloth. Why would she do that if she was working against you?"

Nox turned to Behemoth. "Do you know anything that could be useful to us?"

The goat blinked. "I've been inside a stone in the gem room of the museum for thirty years."

"Is that a no?"

The goat bounced his head again. "It's a no. Can I have a burger soon?"

"Yes," I told him, before looking back to Nox. "Do you think Adstutus will have anything stronger to hide my wings?"

Nox looked over my shoulder at them a long moment, and I could see desire stirring in his eyes. Warmth seeped into my cheeks. "No. Not while you have the stone. I think you shall have to embrace them a while."

"Do you... like them?" I tried not to sound shy and failed. I also avoided looking at the Hell-goat beside him.

"Yes. I do."

The warmth spread down my neck, through my chest, pooling at my core. I believed him. For most of my life, I had only heard the bad stuff when people spoke. I knew that compliments were given just to be polite, and I knew how dull I was, so they meant very little to me. In fact, I barely heard them. But when Nox praised anything about me... I knew it was real. And it lifted me, strengthened me.

I embraced the hit of confidence and leaned into him before it fled. He smelled like wood-smoke and whisky, and I closed my eyes, savoring his scent. "I wonder what they'll look like when they're all I've got on?" I whispered into his ear.

He tensed, sucking in a slow breath. "You are playing with fire, Miss Abbott," he rumbled.

"I know. I'm told I'm getting quite good at it."

He turned his head, ever so slowly. I kept mine exactly where it was, and his lips brushed mine. Hot sparks rushed me, and I barely contained a moan.

"You're becoming a fucking expert," he hissed. Lust magic rolled from him, engulfing me, setting my skin alight with want.

"You're cheating."

"You're irresistible."

Behemoth's voice cut through my sex-addled haze like a douse of cold water. "I'm hungry."

"Fucking Hell-goats," Nox said.

SEVEN

BETH

"Why does the Lord of Hell need to stand in line to get a burger?" Behemoth sounded genuinely confused as the question was projected into my mind.

I saw the corners of Nox's mouth quirk up.

"Because he's not an asshole, and these people were here first," I replied, gesturing to the people in front of us at the market-stall just outside the coffee shop. The smell of hot meat wafted our way, and I had to admit I was quite looking forward to a burger myself. Although I hadn't asked if burgers in magical marketplaces were made of the same thing human burgers were. I decided I'd rather not know.

"What are we doing for the rest of today?" I asked instead, but as I turned to Nox, all thoughts of the day's plans fled. "What's wrong?"

He was completely rigid, and his eyes had turned inky black. His wings burst from his back, the gleaming gold covered in swirling shadows spreading fast across the feathers. "Wrath," he growled.

"What about her?" My heart was instantly hammering against my ribs, anxiety filling me as his power oozed out, making my legs weak. The heat in my chest burned hot, and the now familiar warmth coiled through me, buffering me against the terror rolling from the dark angel before me.

"She's dead."

"Dead?" I half stammered the word. Everyone in the marketplace was staring at Nox. "She can't be. How-How do you know?"

"I am connected to her." An unexpected bolt of jealousy distracted me, until a flash of light drew my attention to my right.

"Gabriel?"

Nox snarled, turning to his brother who had just appeared out of thin air beside him. Gabriel was dressed as I'd seen him before, in shorts and a loose linen shirt, and his long blonde hair was tied back at his neck.

"Michael is in the coffee shop," he said quietly.

"We'll be open again in half an hour, I assure you," came the voice of the waiter from earlier, and I looked over to see that he was holding the coffee shop door open, and the patrons were streaming out into the market, whispering and staring.

Nox glared at them all, and then he and Gabriel

strode into the shop. Behemoth and I looked at each other and followed.

Sitting at the table we had vacated, his big smile totally absent, was Michael. Behemoth made a strange chittering sound as we approached.

"Is that a Hell-goat?" Michael asked, standing. Nox dragged a chair out loudly from the table, and his wings shimmered and vanished.

"Yes." He answered, a ring of steel to his voice. "What has happened to Madaleine?"

"Her body was just found." Gabriel's tone was soft, almost sympathetic.

"At the museum?" My own voice was hoarse, and the two angels snapped their eyes to me.

"How do you know that?"

"I just saw her there. Maybe an hour ago."

"Sit."

I did, choosing the chair next to Nox.

"She was found in the magical part of the museum. In front of the trinity painting."

A violent churning took my stomach, and I swallowed hard. How on earth could a woman like Madaleine be killed? She had borderline superpowers—anybody could feel her strength when they got within a hundred feet of her.

"How was she killed?" Nox asked, clearly thinking the same thing.

"Some sort of beast. And there was evidence of fire."

Nox bared his teeth, a burst of heat accompanying the action. "Hellhounds."

Both Michael and Gabriel nodded.

Michael looked at me. His eyes focused over my shoulders, on my wings. "You had no power when we last saw you."

"Never mind that, we must find out why Wrath was killed," snapped Nox.

"What happens to her power? Has it come back to you?" I asked him.

He shook his head. "No. I need the page. That will be where the power has returned to."

"You may search her house," said Michael.

Nox gave him a sarcastic smile. "Thank you so much for your permission, brother," he half spat.

Electricity filled the air, and a humming sounded in my ears. Behemoth chittered again from under the table.

"What about Cornu?" Everyone looked at me again. "He was with her. Was he killed too?"

Gabriel shook his head. "We found no bodies other than hers."

"He was a demon, if that makes a difference?"

Michael's expression changed to one of distaste. "I know nothing of him." He waved his wrist dismissively. "Obviously the Ward is handling this as a priority, but Lucifer, we want you to find that page. Your power must be returned. Something is at work here, something dangerous to us all."

Nox stared at his brother. "And you truly have no idea what?"

"No. But we can no longer ignore the rise in sinners, and the loss of Saints."

I opened my mouth to ask what Saints were but closed it again. I'd keep my ignorance to myself, at least until Nox and I were alone. My hands were shaking slightly. How could Madaleine be dead? It just didn't seem possible, especially when I'd just seen her. *And the figure in the overcoat following her.*

Much as I longed to throw my questions at the group, the hostility in the air was tangible, and I held my tongue.

"It is your job to keep track of your disciples," said Nox.

Michael banged his fists on the table, making me jump. Normally my heart would have set to racing faster, and I'd have felt cowed by the aggressive action. But instead, fire burst to life in my chest, my spine straightened, and my lips parted in challenge.

I will not be intimidated. The voice was clear in my mind, and it was my own.

"And it is yours to keep the world's balance in check," Michael snarled.

"I chose to disown my job. You're just shit at yours."

There was an abrupt shift in the atmosphere, and for a split second I couldn't breathe as an intense pressure swamped me. I heard Michael shout, Nox growl, and then Gabriel was on his feet and the smell of the ocean powered through the oppressive swampy air, clearing it.

"Enough," he said calmly. "If our foe has moved on to killing angels as strong as Madaleine, then we need to work together."

Heat was pouring from Nox, and despite the fact that he hadn't moved from his chair, every single thing about him promised a world of pain and fire. And it stirred a fierce admiration in me that I was finding impossible to ignore.

I was going to have to face the truth. I was definitely starting to get turned on by the darker side of him. I had no idea how I felt about that, so I pushed the moral questionability to the back of my head and instead drank in every hard plane, every drop of heated fury, every inch of lethal grace. He was beyond beautiful.

"I do not believe Banks stole my book," Nox ground out eventually. "But we know he wants the sin powers."

"So you believe you have two enemies?" Gabriel's voice remained calm and level.

"Yes. And Banks is the weaker of the two. But either could have killed Madaleine to try to take my power or stop me regaining it."

Michael gave a curt nod. He was giving off some pretty strong fuck-off vibes of his own, but they didn't match Nox's. "Find the page. Get your power back. Restore some damn balance to this world."

Nox stood up, shoving his chair back. "Beth," was all he said, before he turned and marched away.

I responded to his summons instantly, only pausing to throw a small nod at Gabriel. The guy had saved my life last time I'd seen him, and seemed significantly less hard work than his brother. I heard Behemoth's hooves clicking behind me but I didn't turn to check, just followed Nox out of the building.

EIGHT

"Arrogant prick," Nox growled as we made our way through Solum. Every single person there was giving him a seriously wide berth, and I was almost having to skip to keep up with him.

"I concur," said Behemoth in my head. Nox glanced down at the little goat, prancing along at my heels. "I don't do very well in the company of archangels, though," he added.

"Most Hell-beings don't," Nox muttered. He didn't need to add *me included* for the implication to be clear.

"What do we do now?" My mind was a jumble. I had questions, and an impulse to act that I was struggling to suppress. Killing Madaleine was taking the fight to a new level, and a restless urgency was seeping into me.

"Home. I need to think." He looked at me, eyes still swirling with light and dark. "And you have questions, no doubt."

. . .

Nox called Rory from the car and told her what happened. Then he called Malc, and put him on speaker-phone. "I need any and all footage you have of Madaleine's movements in the city the last few days. And get me all of her addresses. She's got at least two proper-ties in London, and I think one in Rome."

"And Cornu," I added. "Look for Cornu."

"Her demon toy-boy?" Malc said.

"Yes."

"If you say so, Lady Boss."

It was lunchtime when we got to Nox's, and my stomach rumbled loudly as we entered the hallway, reminding me that we hadn't actually got our burgers. I still felt shaky and uneasy, adrenaline from being present at an alterca-tion between three of the most powerful beings in London still flowing through me. Nox glanced at me and pulled his cellphone out again.

"Pizza?"

Both Behemoth and I nodded enthusiastically.

We settled in the sitting room, pizza on plates on our laps. Behemoth consented to eat his from a plate on the floor, thank god.

It didn't take long for the food to make my stomach feel better and the adrenaline to lessen as I absorbed the calm of Nox's house. If he was still angry, then he was containing it well; a thoughtful seriousness had settled over him during the drive home.

"You made Michael mad over something to do with Saints. What is a Saint?" I asked.

"Saints are just good angels. There are two types of angels. Well, three, actually. All angels are created with the magic of the realm they come from, Heaven or Hell. Fallen angels are created from Hell magic, and Saints are created from Heavenly magic."

I looked at Behemoth, remembering what he said about being made from Hell magic. "What's the difference between a Hell-creature and an angel from Hell?"

"Angels have their magic encased in a human being. Demons, or Hell-goats, or even Gods, for that matter, are pure magical energy. A Fallen angel or a Saint is human at heart. That's why angels run this world and created the Veil here. And why angels live and procreate with humans. They link magic with humanity."

I swallowed before asking my next question, unsure I wanted to hear the answer. "Are you human at heart?"

He gave me a wicked smile. "Yes. But I'm special. I'm the third type of angel. And there are only three of us."

"The painting," I breathed.

He nodded. "I was created in balance with my brothers, and because Hell magic is so corruptive, there needed to be twice as much Heavenly magic. We are Archangels, and we have power over all who use our magic. We were created to preside over our respective magics."

"You can control anyone with Hell magic?"

"Except a god, yes. If they have the magic of my

realm, I am their Lord. And my brothers can control Saints, who use Heavenly magic."

I thought for a minute. "Michael said something about losing Saints?"

"Yes. Angels of Kindness, Hope, Selflessness, Honesty - all sorts of virtuous powers, have been diminishing over the last few years."

"I feel this too," piped up Behemoth. "There is less good in London than when I was last here."

"How do you mean, diminishing?" I asked. "Like less are being created?"

Nox took a bite of pizza, then answered. "We're not sure. We don't keep track of actual beings, just the amount of power we can feel. The energy from sinners and fallen angels is outweighing that of the energy from the Saints more each year." He shrugged. "I know nothing of my brother's angels. I meant what I said to Michael, the Saints are his problem."

We ate in silence for a few moments. "Do you think they are right about a Hellhound being involved in Madaleine's death?" I asked. "Because I thought I saw someone following her today, in the museum, and I think they were at the retirement home yesterday too."

Nox snapped his head up. "Were you alone? What happened?"

"Nothing, and it might just be coincidence. Francis and I saw someone in the gardens, where we'd just been working out, wearing a beige overcoat. But they left when I got closer. I saw someone in the same coat today, at the museum. But it's hardly a rare kind of coat, and there were lots of people in the museum."

Shadows flickered in his eyes. "Could it have been Banks?"

"No. They were a smaller build. Honestly, it's probably nothing. Especially if a Hellhound killed Madaleine."

"Madaleine should have been stronger than a Hellhound. Shit, she should have been stronger than most Hell-beings." Nox ground his teeth, closed his eyes a second, and then spoke. "We need to go to her home and see if we can find any indication of where the Wrath page is."

"Do you think she found it?"

"I don't believe she ever sold it. The woman had power and money, and no reason to let go of something that precious to her."

I remembered her refusing to admit that she had tried to destroy the Wrath page, even though it was clear that she had. She had been desperate to keep her sin power, so keeping the page in her control did seem more likely than selling it on, especially if she didn't need the money.

"Do you think that was what she was killed for?"

"I can't think of any other reason. Although she may have had her own enemies."

"I guess she didn't have it on her when she died, or Michael and Gabriel would have found it."

Nox made a hissing sound. "They wouldn't necessarily give it to me."

"They really seem to want you to get your power

back," I said slowly. I needed to choose my words carefully when it came to his brothers.

"Outwardly, yes. But Beth, do not underestimate the gulf between us. They were created from light, and I dark. They despise me on a level so deep they can't control it."

I thought about the two angels. Michael was hard to read, and I strongly suspected he was keeping something from Nox. But Gabriel...

"I think Gabriel cares for you."

"That is what he wants you to think." Nox's whole demeanor turned stormy. "You owe him nothing." A primal growl slipped into his tone.

That wasn't true - I owed Gabriel my life. But I nodded all the same. "I know." I leaned forward, touching my lips to his cheek. "I'm yours."

His shoulders relaxed, and he turned his head, catching my lips with his. "Mine," he murmured against me, the soft skin caressing mine.

I leaned back, taking a deep breath and trying to calm my heating body. "Madaleine's house," I said.

Nox nodded, and I could see he was restraining himself too. "Let's see if she really did keep the page."

NINE

BETH

adaleine's apartment looked exactly like I thought it would.

White.

Everything was white. The walls, ceiling, floor tiles, kitchen counter, couch - everything.

"Wow. I don't think I could live somewhere with so little color," I breathed as I followed Nox around the small space. We were in one of the most expensive areas of London, Hyde Park Corner, and this tiny studio apartment probably cost the same as an entire block of apartments where I lived.

"I don't think she lived here," Nox said, opening a closet door and looking inside.

"No?"

"No. I think this is where she brought people. The white was to keep her calm. She must have somewhere else she went to let go."

It was weird, looking around the home of someone

who had just been murdered. Someone I had seen and spoken to just an hour before they got murdered.

I shuddered.

Madaleine hadn't woken up that morning aware she was going to die. When she'd spoken to me by the dinosaur skeleton, she'd had no idea she was about to lose her life.

I looked over at Nox, heart beating a little harder. Should we throw caution to the wind? Should we live like there might be no tomorrow? Or was that just my desperate lust for Nox trying to justify doing something stupid?

Nox looked back at me, eyes bright, and I wondered if he was thinking the same thing. "There's nothing here," he said gruffly. "Let's go."

"Where to now?" I asked when we climbed back into the car. Nox lifted a piece of paper from his pocket, and his arm brushed mine. Tingles rippled across my skin, making my hairs stand on end, and he paused. He turned a little on the leather seat, bringing his hand up and pulling my face to his.

"I want you."

His breath whispered across my lips before they closed hungrily over mine.

"I want you too," I told him breathlessly when he moved back. And boy, was it true. I ached for him.

"We need to find one of these fucking sins soon," he growled. I nodded, pointing to the paper.

"Where next?" Maybe we'll get lucky and she put the page in a piggy bank. Or a safe." I frowned. "Although, we might have trouble getting into a safe."

The hunger in Nox's face was evident when he spoke. "I'll melt a safe to the damn ground, if it means I can fuck you."

I shifted in my seat, trying to move away from him. It was that or I wouldn't be able to stop myself from mounting him, which was a bad idea for a number of reasons - not least that Claude was up front, waiting for directions, and Behemoth was waiting less patiently to be let into the car.

With a last, burning, look at me, Nox reached forward and passed the piece of paper through the hatch to the cab. "This is the next address from Malcolm," he barked.

I leaned out of the car door and helped Behemoth in.

"Right away, Sir," I heard Claude say, and the car pulled away.

The house we pulled up at looked nothing like the fancy apartment we'd just come from. At least, not from the outside. It was in Shoreditch, a trendy part of London full of creative types and independent businesses. The bottom floor, like most in the city, was shop-space. Unlike most buildings in the city though, this house was detached, with clear alleyways on both sides.

"Dizzy's Dry Cleaners," I read aloud as we got out of the car. Nox looked between the two alleyways and picked the one with a dumpster in it. A black door with a modern white archway framing it was set in the red brick, and it was ajar.

"Which apartment is hers?" I asked as we began to climb the stairs. There were four floors above the shop, so there were probably a few in the building. I hadn't seen an intercom or mailbox though.

"Malcolm's note didn't say."

At the top of the stairs was another black door, and when Nox tried the handle, it was locked. There was no number on the door, or any other doors to try.

"Do you think the whole thing is hers?"

"Perhaps."

"Can you unlock it?"

He turned, giving me his most mischievous smile. My tummy swooped a little, and heat radiated from him. The door clicked, and he turned the handle.

As far as I could see, there was no white in this place at all. It was almost as though she'd gone out of her way to avoid it. I was reminded of an alpine lodge as I wandered through the super opulent lounge. A giant L shaped couch in a rich chocolate brown dominated the room, facing a huge log fire. A flat-screen TV was mounted on the right-hand wall, and a long redwood bookcase with a bar in the center filled the left.

"This is nice," I said. The floors were wood, and most of the upholstery was a duck-egg blue. It was warm and cozy and stylish. "Really nice."

Nox was at the bookcase, moving books and looking behind them. "Help me look."

I joined him, and together we went through the huge unit, while Behemoth sniffed around the room, hooves clicking. When we found nothing, we moved to the staircase at the back of the room. The next floor up was a kitchen, and it was equally as warm and inviting as the living room had been.

We systematically checked through all the drawers, the stack of recipe books, every cupboard. There was no sign of the sin page.

The next floor up was a bedroom, and it felt more like Madaleine than the other two floors did. Not because there was anything white though. The opposite in fact. The whole room was black, even the ceiling. Plush bedding covered the gargantuan bed, and soft velours and silks hung everywhere, giving the room a very feminine vibe. A very dark feminine vibe.

Nox didn't hesitate to move to the closet. I took a second to swallow back my discomfort at the invasion of privacy and went to check the nightstand. All I could find were the sorts of things all women kept there; a book, hair ties, a Chapstick.

"Nothing here," said Nox. I turned to him, my eyes widening when I saw what he was standing in front of. It was a closet full of the skimpiest outfits I'd ever seen. Somehow they managed to be as inappropriate as something worn at the Aphrodite Club, and yet look exceedingly expensive.

I felt an irrational bolt of jealousy as I thought about

Madaleine wearing any of them, realizing Nox would probably have thought about the same thing whilst going through them.

She would look a thousand times better in any one of them than I would.

"Do you-" I started to say, then stopped. I had been about to ask Nox if he would want me to wear things like that. But I didn't finish the question, because if he said yes, I didn't know if I had the guts to actually do it.

And besides, we couldn't have sex anyway. Not until he got his power back, became the full devil again, and went to live in Hell - where we *also* wouldn't be able to have sex because I was mortal and didn't want to live in actual Hell.

I folded my arms, unable to keep the angry sigh from escaping me.

"What's wrong?"

"Nothing. There's one more floor."

I knew it wasn't his fault, but I didn't want to talk about it. Especially not here, in a dead woman's home.

With a small, concerned glance at me, he headed toward the stairs.

I was not prepared for what was on the top floor.

"Jeeeeeez," I said on hiss of breath.

The room was a penthouse freaking dungeon.

One wall was covered with whips, flogs, and what looked like a riding crop. Another wall had a cross and shackles, along with a few other things I didn't recognize.

The whole room was done in red and black, with a large bed taking up most of the space and a long leather padded table at the foot of it.

"I am not searching through this stuff." I re-folded my arms, and Nox's smile turned as wicked as it got. His eyes shone, and his Lust power rolled over me. Heat, both my own and from the ball of power, fluttered through me.

"Does this stuff make you uncomfortable?"

I looked around at it all, trying to work out what my answer was.

Uncomfortable? *Yes.*

Curious? *Also yes.*

"It's not something I am familiar with."

Nox made a tutting sound. "And here I was thinking you were a reader of romance books."

"With cowboys and firefighters! Not..." I gave up trying to find the right words and waved my arms around the room. "This!" I scowled at him, wishing my cheeks weren't as red as I knew they were. "I'm assuming it doesn't make you uncomfortable?"

His eyes locked on mine, and I swear I could see his desires playing out in my head like a movie. Or were they my desires?

Shit.

When he spoke, his voice was liquid honey, the promise of sex in every damn syllable. "I like a measure of... control."

A pulse of need hit me, and my eyes went straight to a red velvet swing with two sets of restraints hanging from its chains. I swallowed hard at the image that rose in my mind. I was sure I could feel his heat sizzling on my skin as he spoke.

"In fact," he said, his voice now a growl, "I like to take complete control." His heat was making me sweat. "But for you, I would make an exception."

"It's hot," I blurted out.

He stared at me a beat before speaking again. "I think a dip in the pool is what you need."

TEN

BETH

"I don't think this is a good idea," I said, as Nox unbuttoned his shirt.

He hadn't been kidding. As soon as we got back to his place, he'd told Behemoth to stay in the kitchen, on pain of death, and led me straight upstairs, to the pool on the roof deck.

To be fair, it was a hot day, too hot for the time of year, but I knew that wasn't why he wanted to get in the pool.

"It's a great idea." He dropped his shirt to the ground, and I bit my lip hard. Sculpted like a damn statue, I watched transfixed as his hands moved to his belt.

"I don't have any swimming stuff."

"I know."

I blew out a long breath. I could feel the moisture building between my legs just watching him take his freaking clothes off. There was no question where this was going to end up.

"Seriously, Nox. We can't."

He dropped his pants to the tiles. My whole body tightened.

His underwear was tight, his erection straining against it.

"Beth, if I don't get a taste of you soon, I'm going to fucking explode," he growled. "And that's more dangerous than losing a little power. I need you."

"I don't want to hurt you."

God I wanted him. The idea that he might actually be about to touch me sent shivers running across my skin.

"Get in the damn pool."

In a swift move, he pulled down his underwear. A tiny moan escaped me at the sight of him, and then I was practically tearing my own clothes off. He watched me, his body so tense he could have been made of rock.

A slight breeze skimmed across the rooftop, making my nipples harden and the heat between my thighs feel even more intense.

Nox drew in a breath, then dropped down into the pool, the movement graceful. I followed him in.

"Come here." The smooth timbre of his voice was a siren song, enough to draw me to him without thinking.

I closed the distance between us, my breath coming short.

We were actually doing this.

I knew how good this would feel and anticipation, combined with a primal need, was making my stomach flip.

"Stop," he commanded.

I did, half a foot from him. He reached out, slowly, circling his wet finger under my breasts, drinking them in with his bright eyes. He flicked his fingertips over my nipple, and I exhaled hard.

He took a small step closer. "Will you do as I tell you?"

I was about to say yes, but something stopped me. The images from the sex room swam through my mind; me tied up on the table, restrained in the swing, bent over the edge of the bed, laid across his knees...

"Why don't you do what I tell you?" My voice was barely a whisper, and I straightened my shoulders, trying to instill confidence in the words. The action drew his attention back to my breasts, and his eyelids dipped with desire.

He dropped his head, brushing his lips against mine, then nipping my bottom lip.

I gasped, my muscles clenching at the unexpected sensation.

"What do you have in mind? Tell me what you want. Say it for me," he whispered into the wet length of my hair as he drew me tight into him. I reveled in the clutch of his fingers digging deep into my flesh. His erection pressed into my stomach, hard and huge and enough to make my mind blank.

It took me clearing my throat to be able to give him an answer. "I want to pleasure you."

He pulled away enough to look down into my face. Desire burned in his eyes.

I blinked up at him, wishing I had the courage to lay it out in excruciating detail. That I had the ability to bring him to the brink with just my words, my voice, like he could for me. "I want to taste you," is all I managed of a litany of things I really wanted to do to him.

He gently guided me backward by the elbows, parting the water with my body until my back hit the smooth tiles of the pool's edge. When I was pressed completely between the hard tiles and his solid body, he cupped my ass in his hands and lifted me up to sit.

"I said I want to pleasure you," I managed to get out before his full lips closed around my right nipple. My ability to articulate became hazy, and he flicked his tongue across my sensitive skin, the heat of his mouth so in contrast with the cool air swirling around me.

The sharp edge of his teeth came next, and I cried out, both pleasure and pain in one.

His lips moved down my stomach, sensation firing out from every contact.

"You're so beautiful," he hissed as he reached my thighs, slowly parting them.

"Nox, please," I said, begging with both my words and my body, my fingers digging into his arms as they gripped my thighs. I ached all over with desire, and I knew he must be able to see how much I wanted him as he stared down at me.

"What are you begging for, Beth?" His words pulled every hint of arousal tighter in my body, like a string yanked taut.

"You."

"Specifically?"

His lips brushed against my heat.

"That," I half choked.

"Say it."

I dragged my resolve back, and pressed my thighs back together, forcing him back.

I swallowed hard before I looked down at him. "I want to taste you."

His eyes darkened, then he stepped backward. I slid back into the water, and he gripped my hips and lifted me as he rotated us, hungry, dark eyes still locked on mine. When he had swapped positions so that his back was to the pool edge, he set me back down.

Slowly, he hauled himself up out of the water. When all his glorious skin came into view, I relearned every curve, every muscle, every water-slicked inch of him I wanted to put my mouth on. That's what I wanted. Him in my mouth so I could inspire in him even an ounce of what he had awakened in me.

I groaned aloud at the sight of him. The long length of his cock stood tall against the planes of his ab muscles and my mind blanked again as I lost myself in drinking the sight of him in.

His voice shook me from my reverie. "You had plans for me?"

I nodded. Suddenly nervous, I reached out and wrapped my hand around his length. His skin was flushed and hot under my grip, and my own desire made my knees weak.

"You wanted to taste me," he said from above, his voice low and impossibly sexy. Confidence surged through me.

I leaned in and clamped my lips around the dusky head of his cock. He jerked lightly in my hold but stilled as I began to move. His hand slid into my wet hair, pulling the strands hard and tight into his fist.

"Don't stop." The words were a plea and an order rolled into one.

I sank my mouth around him, drawing him deeper into the back of my throat. His groan goaded me on, giving me the courage to add a little more suction into the mix.

The more he reacted to me, the more my body fired hot, liquid need pooling further between my legs.

He began to move with me, and I couldn't tell who was in charge anymore. With one hand on the back of my hair, guiding my head, and the other cupping my cheek he gently fucked my mouth, never going any further than the back of my throat. I swallowed against him, trying to draw him deeper, take him harder, make it last longer, but he kept gentling the touch I tried to roughen.

His fingers tightened on my face, and I gently pulled my mouth off him. My jaw ached from my efforts, and his additions, but I didn't care. Once I readjusted my stance and my hands to grip him right at the base, I delved down to take him into my mouth again. This time, I was determined to drag his entire length down the back of my throat.

"Easy," he whispered, his fingers still tangled in my

wet hair. But I didn't want to go easy. I wanted him rabid for me.

I sucked harder, using my tongue, the soft scrape of my teeth over his crown, even my hands when I drew them up to meet my lips along his length. It wasn't long until I'd opened enough to take him harder, the blunt tip of his cock hitting the back of my throat. The first time I succeeded in swallowing it he let out a strangled sigh and jerked away in reflex, but I wouldn't let him go.

A heartbeat of arousal had taken root in me, and I wanted him inside me more than anything. But this... this was for him, and all the pleasure he'd given me so far.

I sucked him down hard again, swallowing once more to draw his length in the back of my throat. His hand convulsed in my hair, and then the hot jet of him coming followed. It filled the back of my throat and I swallowed on reflex, extending his pleasure and my own by default. When he stopped shuddering against me, he gently eased his fingers from my hair to then cupped my cheeks in both hands to pull me away.

"Fuck," he rasped.

I stared up at him, panting. His eyes were wild, his cock still hard and throbbing.

He slid into the pool, wrapping has arms tight around me. I lifted my legs in the water as he took my weight, wrapping them around him on instinct. When he felt my wetness against him he growled. His lips met mine, and when he kissed me, images exploded into my head. Every drop of pleasure I'd just given him rushed through me, and without even realizing what I was doing, I was shifting around him, trying to let his straining erection meet my molten core.

When I finally got to the right spot, feeling him against my entrance, he kissed me harder.

"You're in control," he said against my lips.

I sank down onto him, my thighs squeezing hard around him.

He exhaled deeply, pulling me tighter against his chest, and moving a hand down to cup my ass.

Slowly, he lifted me.

I was made for him. It was the only thought in my head as perfect pleasure rocketed through every nerve ending in my body.

He bounced me up and down his length, slowly at first, and then faster. I was pressed so tight to him that my clit rubbed against his base, and in what seemed like no time at all, the pleasure intensified, knotting in my center.

I kissed him harder, digging my nails into his shoulders.

All the pent-up need spilled over, and my whole body convulsed against him as pleasure ripped through me in a tidal wave. My orgasm triggered him, and I felt him jerk as he pressed hard into me, gripping me tight and grinding his hips against mine.

"Beth," he said his lips still snatching kisses from me as we gasped for breath.

"Nox."

He pushed his hand along my jaw, into my hair, pulling me back to gaze at me.

"You're mine."

"I'm yours."

ELEVEN

BETH

The next morning, the tinny sound of a smartphone ringtone dragged me from the best sleep I'd had in days.

"It's yours," I heard Nox mumble, his arm tight around me in the plush bed. I groped for my phone in the gloom. I closed my hand around it and looked groggily at the screen. It was seven a.m.

"Malc?"

"Morning. Listen, my friend in South America has found something. It's late where she is, but she can get on a video call and explain it to you now, before she goes to bed. Are you available?"

I was instantly awake. "Give me five minutes."

I couldn't stop fidgeting as I stared at Nox's laptop screen. I was trying desperately not to get my hopes up, but it was hard. I wanted so badly to know more about my parents, and without them here to ask, this was surely the best shot I had. But I had become painfully used to being disappointed by lack of information about my parents when I had been searching for them all that time, and I wasn't keen to set myself up for that all-too-familiar sinking-stomach feeling yet again.

Behemoth had asked no questions about the previous night, thank god, and was now sitting on the floor, chewing messily on a Weetabix I'd given him.

When the video call app flared to life, I sat up straight, pressing the answer button quickly. Nox reached out and closed a hand over my knee.

"Boss, Lady Boss," Malc nodded at us both. "This is Nina." A third box appeared on the screen and a striking woman with her hair in a brightly colored scarf waved cheerily at us.

"Good day to you," she said.

"Hello," I smiled nervously back. Nox lifted one hand.

"Rather than me try to relay everything Nina has to say, I thought it would be easier to just patch her in," said Malc.

"I appreciate it," I said, unable to keep my nerves from my voice. "What did you find out?"

"Firstly, it's definitely angel DNA."

My breath caught a little. Nox had believed that was the most likely scenario, but to have it confirmed was still surreal.

"What are your parents' names?" Nina asked me.

"George, and Gloria." She scrawled on her notepad, nodding.

"I believe only one of your parents was an angel, and the bloodwork suggests that it was probably the male side."

"Dad." My word came out a whisper, and I felt my throat tighten.

My parents had always seemed an odd match to me, Mom so strict and careful and serious, and dad so optimistic and cheerful and sensitive. If I'd have had to guess which one of them was an actual angel, I wasn't sure I would have picked Dad, but when I thought about it, he had been an angel to me my whole life. Years of missing him threatened to overwhelm me, and the backs of my eyes prickled.

Nina looked warmly at me. "Yes. And there was enough trace for me to narrow down what kind of angel he was."

"A Saint," I breathed.

She nodded. "Yes. His power is either Hope or Joy. The signature of both magics are very similar so I can't be sure which."

A tear spilled as memories tumbled unbridled through my mind. It was as though a lifetime of experience was solidifying into something I felt like I'd known forever.

All the times he had refilled the emotional well of the people around him and offered never-ending encouragement to those who were failing. Especially me. Dad never gave up on anyone.

Nox squeezed my hand hard but said nothing. Nina continued to smile at me. "You must miss him."

All I could do was nod at her, my throat too tight to speak without a sob escaping.

I was no closer to finding my parents, and I had no more information about whether they were alive or not. But years of grief were bubbling up from where the debilitating emotion had been buried. My whole childhood, my teens, all those years spent with my parents, and they never told me that dad was an angel. He was a Saint, with Heavenly magic, making people happy or giving them hope.

I felt fiercely proud of him, and utterly betrayed at the same time, and the resulting confusion was making it impossible for me to concentrate on the faces on the laptop.

"Boss, Nina thinks she may have a book somewhere that could help with that symbol too," Malc was saying. I tried to focus on him through blurry eyes.

"Yes, I recognize part of it. I believe it is dark magic, and I think it has to do with the control of beasts."

Nox stiffened next to me. "Could it be how someone is controlling Hellhounds?"

Nina looked thoughtful, then nodded. "Yes. That's a definite possibility. It's a very ancient symbol, and if it was being used to control a feral creature from Hell then it would have to be imbued with some seriously dark magic."

"Who could do that?" Malc asked.

"Madaleine would have been able to," Nox muttered.

"Could a Hellhound have turned on her if something went wrong?"

"Perhaps," said Nina. "I'll dig into my books and confirm whether the symbol could be connected to the Hellhounds. And Beth?"

I blinked at her on the screen. "Yes?"

"Heavenly magic is powerful. Or at least, it used to be. There's a very good chance your parents are still alive. It takes a lot to put down Hope and Joy."

"Thank you," I whispered. Her smiling face vanished from the screen, Nox thanked Malc and closed the lid of the laptop. But I barely registered the movement. Her words were spinning through my head on repeat, and my heart began skipping in my chest. A thought was forming in my head, a feeling like cogs turning, turning, turning, before slotting into place exactly where they should be.

Heavenly magic is powerful. Or at least, it used to be.

My hand shook slightly as I turned my head. "Nox, my parents went missing five years ago, and we now know one of them was a Saint." His eyes locked on mine, filled with indecipherable emotion. "What if they were part of this *diminishing* of Saint magic? What if someone took them?"

Nox stared at me. "You're saying someone has been abducting angels?"

"Is it possible?"

"They would have to be extremely powerful. It would be no easy feat to kidnap angels."

"It's no easy feat to kill Madaleine, but someone did!" I objected. His face tightened, and I realized what he was thinking. "If they are capable of abducting angels, then they are probably capable of killing them too." I felt sick as I said it.

"Maybe. But we found Madaleine's body. As far as I'm aware, no Saints have been found dead over the years. They just slowly...lessened in power and presence." His voice turned thoughtful, and his thumb brushed reassuringly up my forearm.

"Why would someone abduct good angels?" I asked quietly. I didn't know if I wanted to be right or not, but I couldn't shift the certainty I felt. It made so much sense. This couldn't all be coincidence.

"Either just to make the world an unhappier place, or in preparation for something more specific."

"Like what?"

Nox thought a long moment, before speaking. "The Ward have blamed the increase in sinners on me failing to deliver punishment. What if the increase in sinners is actually due to the loss of Joy, Honesty, Kindness, and the other Heavenly magic that Saints bring to the world? What if this invisible foe we have been fighting is behind this?"

"They've been kidnapping Saints to make you look bad? Who would do that?"

"Somebody who wanted to remove me from power. If Michael and Gabriel believed I was responsible for the human world collapsing into sin, then they would have grounds to take my power from me. And they are the only beings who can do so."

"Why not just kill you? Why go through years of kidnapping people to get the Ward to do it for them?"

"Politics. Killing me, even outright attacking me, would start a war. I'm the treasured pet of Examinus, one of the most lethal beings ever created." Shadows filled his eyes as he spoke, hatred oozing from him. This anger wasn't like the dark strength he'd exuded with his brothers that had made my whole body heat. It was something deeper, and dark enough that I was forced to drop his gaze.

I let out a long breath. "What changed then? Assuming this is correct, and someone spent years slowly working to have you taken down by abducting Saints and blaming you, why suddenly steal the book and pages now?"

"You."

My stomach clenched as I found his intense gaze again.

"I now have a very good reason to reclaim my power and lift my curse. And I would be much, much harder to remove from power at full strength. My assailant no longer has the luxury of time."

I had no idea what to say. Could it be true? Could my parents have been taken as part of a plot against Nox?

Or was I way, way off base, and they were just killed in a car accident five years ago, and never found?

I felt the backs of my eyes burn again, emotion threatening to overwhelm me. "Nox, I need a little time. Just to, you know, work this out." His eyes were full of something I didn't recognize, though the closest guess I had was worry. I didn't know whether it was the subject of Examinus, the realization that there might a plot against him, or just my own emotion that was causing it. "It's hard to explain, but grieving for my parents is a process I've been in for a long time. It's sort of... mine. I need to be in my own place and see Francis. Not because you don't make me feel better - you do - I just-"

He cut me off, planting a soft kiss on my lips, halting my words, and relief rushed me. "I understand."

"Thank you."

TWELVE

I watched Beth and the little Hell-goat make their way to Claude's car, a rising feeling of unease gripping me as she moved farther away.

If it were up to me, I wouldn't let her more than a foot from my side. But it couldn't be like that. More than I wanted my own happiness, I wanted Beth to become who she was meant to be. I needed her to know how strong she was. I needed her to embrace her own company, her own thoughts. Eventually she would love and trust herself enough to dispel all the shitty self-doubt and pain she carried with her.

The thought of her being in pain made anger spark in my gut, and I slammed the door closed.

We had to find her parents. Whether they were alive or not, she needed to know. And I would be here. She would not deal with it alone. Not this time.

I marched downstairs to the gym.

Her father was a Saint.

The irony was not lost on me. A fucking Saint. The only woman the devil was capable of loving was the product of an angel of Hope or Joy. The literal antithesis of my own power.

She wasn't an angel though. She was good and kind and selfless, but she was corruptible.

My goal was not to corrupt her, But Hell... Hell would destroy her, piece by piece.

Beth was mortal and raised with the magic of a Saint. There was no denying it. If I had to return to Hell, she could not go with me.

The one woman I could spend my eternal fucking life with, and she couldn't exist by my side. I felt my skin heat as anger made my muscles swell.

I ripped my shirt off and lay down on the weight bench, and an unpleasant thought occurred to me.

The curse.

What if the reason Beth was able to defy the curse, and my body physically responded to her in the way that it did was *because* she was so out of bounds? Could it be another cruel trick woven into the magic Examinus used to fuck me over?

What if the way I felt about her was part of Examinus' punishment? What if the curse itself was always going to make me fall for the offspring of a Saint? Someone who would either kill me through sex, or leave me broken and alone because they couldn't live with me after my power was restored? It was a vicious punishment.

I snarled as I lifted the barbell loaded with weights, and felt a satisfying pain burn through my biceps.

My feelings for Beth were real, not part of the curse. They had to be.

Didn't they?

"Fucking Examinus," I hissed, as I slammed the barbell back down. "Arrogant, cruel, asshole god."

A chuckle filtered through my head, and I froze. *"Use my name, little one, and I may hear you."*

Examinus' voice was a knife through my skull, sharp and painful.

"Get out of my head."

"You would prefer to visit with me in Hell?"

"Because that went so well last time," I spat, ducking under my barbell and sitting up.

"You are weak, Lucifer. The girl weakens you."

"Lift my curse, and I'll get the sins back."

"Lies."

"I'll be able to get them back if I am not this weak. Lift the curse."

"You wouldn't be so weak if you didn't repeatedly succumb to your desires. Weak of mind, weak of body."

"Why her? Was that your doing?"

"I wouldn't tell you if it was, Lucifer. Kill yourself for pleasure, or return to full strength and live your life basking in the true magnificence you are capable of. Those are your options."

Beth's' words, her insistence that I should try to negotiate with the god, crept through my frustration. "You know I do not wish to reside in Hell, spending endless hours with scum. I will do exactly as you ask, if you help me find another way to live."

Another chuckle clawed its way through my brain. *"A way to live with the girl? You do not wish to be apart from her."*

"I do not wish to reside in Hell," I repeated. "Just as I didn't seventy years ago. That has not changed."

"She can live here with you."

"No."

"I will turn her into something else for you - a Hell creature of course. Maybe a demon?"

Fear had me on my feet in seconds, flames firing across my skin as my wings burst unbidden from my shoulders. "You fucking dare-"

Pain tore through me, and I doubled over, my wings coiling around me defensively but unable to keep the agony out.

"I dare do whatever I wish, Lucifer. Get your power back and return to Hell. Or I will turn the little mortal into my own personal pet demon."

THIRTEEN

BETH

"Lavender Oaks, please Claude," I said as I helped Behemoth onto a seat in the back of the car.

"You know, it's most undignified getting into this vehicle, but once I'm in I think it's quite fitting for a Hell-beast," he told me. "Where are we going?"

"To see my best friend. I need to tell her what I've found out, so that I can work out how I feel about it."

The goat tilted his furry head. "How you feel about it? Surely you need to find the unholy urchin who kidnapped your father and unleash hell upon their person?"

I raised my eyebrows at him. "You think that's what happened then? You think my parents were taken?"

"From what I have heard, I think that it seems likely. What is not likely is you and Lucifer."

"What do you mean?"

"You are the offspring of a Saint. He is the Lord of the Fallen. That is a bad match."

A new sick feeling joined the existing one in my stomach. "A bad match," I repeated. Was that what that look in Nox's eyes had been? He couldn't love the offspring of a Saint? His kiss had said otherwise, but I had never seen that look before.

"You represent the opposite of his power."

"*I'm* not an angel," I said, so insistently I surprised myself. "I have none of my father's power."

My words faltered as I said *father*, the memory of him once again hitting me square in the gut.

"Why are you sad to learn this of your parents?"

"Lots of reasons. They kept so much from me. I miss them. I'm angry with them for lying to me. I'm desperate to see them again." New tears crept down my cheek and I gritted my teeth. "I hope they are not in pain, or worse."

Behemoth cocked his head the other way, assessing me. "That sounds complicated. I am glad Hell-goats do not have to manage such conflicting emotions."

"Yeah."

"But you should not be sad. You have the Lord of Hell at your side. There is no other being who is more likely to help you find your lost parents or defeat your foes." He had a point. "And if you are correct, then you seek the same foe. Which is even better." Another good point. Who knew the goat could talk so much sense?

In fact, the more I thought about it, as the car chugged through London traffic toward Wimbledon, the more sense it made. If we were right about mom and dad being taken by the same person who wanted to remove Nox from power, then for the first time ever, I actually had a lead on their disappearance. And even better, it was a lead we were already chasing down.

Behemoth was right. I should not be sad. This was the best news I had received about my parents since they vanished.

An almost excited resolve began to take me in its grip, and my tears dried up completely as the heat in my chest spread, fierce and bold and defiant.

Together, Nox and I would find out who was behind this, and as the little Hell-goat had so succinctly put it - we would defeat our foe.

"Honey, I don't mean to alarm you, but I think you have company." Francis sat up straight in her recliner, her eyes wide and fixed near my feet. I looked down at Behemoth, trotting along at my side, then back up at Francis.

"Can you see him?" Excitement skipped through me. Had Rory actually gotten the Veil lifted for my friend?

"If by him, you mean a black goat with gold horns, then yes." Her words were guarded, and she was scrabbling to get up from her chair.

"Yes! This is Behemoth. He's a Hell-goat."

Francis stopped moving. "Hell-goat? You mean... You mean, I can see a magic thing?"

I grinned as I nodded. "Rory is outside, you should be able to see her too."

She gave a little shriek as she clapped her hands

together, earning some scowls from the other patrons in the retirement house recreational room.

"Come on."

We made our way out to the gardens. I had called Rory from the car and asked her if we could work out. Fresh energy was coursing through me now, the dregs of my sadness replaced with burning restlessness, and a sparring session was exactly what I needed.

"So, you're from Hell? What's that like? Is it hot? And full of lava? And monsters? How long are you here for?" Francis was firing a barrage of questions at Behemoth, who was prancing a little more elegantly than usual and shaking his furry head each time he answered her.

He was loving the attention.

As I tried to stop myself from listening to his answers, I realized why I hadn't asked him a lot of this stuff myself. *I didn't want to know about Hell.* I was avoiding the fact that the man I was falling in love with was the freaking devil, and being with him meant living in Hell.

"My dad was an angel of Hope or Joy," I said, abruptly, cutting off Behemoth's diatribe.

Francis had just lowered herself onto the garden bench, and she looked up at me. "Hope or Joy?"

"Yes."

"Your dad was a Saint?" I spun at Rory's voice. She was just reaching us, wearing yoga pants and a cropped top.

Francis squealed, then leaped up from her bench, thrusting her hand out. "Hello!"

Rory frowned, tilted her head, sighed, and took her hand. "Hi."

"Thanks for lifting the Veil for her," I said.

Rory shrugged. "Whatever."

"A pixie and a Hell-goat, all in one day," beamed Francis.

"Wait till I take you back to the Aphrodite Club and you see all the magic folk there," I teased.

Her face lit up, and I instantly regretted my words. She would actually make me take her. "Beth, did you know that you have small gold wings?"

"Yes. They're from Nox's power."

"Oh, the sex power?"

I blushed as Rory and Behemoth looked at me. "Yes," I hissed at her.

"What does he think about your dad being an angel of Hope or Joy? That's a bit different to his power, isn't it?"

Rory gave a snort. "Saints and the Fallen are like bananas and bacon. They do *not* go together."

I felt a flash of anger at her words, the same feeling I was getting whenever anyone suggested Nox and I couldn't be together. "My dad is the angel, not me. Anyway, Nox and my dad would get on great."

I had no idea if that was true. My strict, Catholic mother would likely pass out if she knew I'd had sex with the devil. One look at that wicked smile of his, and she would lose her shit. Dad, on the other hand, liked everyone.

Fierce hope that they were still alive somewhere, and that they might actually be able to meet Nox one day flooded me. *Hope.* The emotion itself sparked something new inside me. Dad being an angel of Hope seemed more likely to me than Joy. He may not have passed me his angel power, but he'd brought me up with plenty of hope, and I felt a bit like I was truly recognizing it for the first time.

I looked between Rory and Francis. "We think that somebody has been removing good angels from this world for years. Maybe to make it look like *Nox* was causing the imbalance of good and bad in the world."

Rory raised her eyebrows, her lips pursing in thought. "You know, that might make sense."

I nodded. "My parents went missing five years ago."

"Why would they have taken your mom, if she's human?" Francis asked.

"I don't know." Fear that Mom might have been a loose end filled me, and I shook off the thought, clinging to my new determination. "But it means if we find out who is trying to stop Nox getting his power back, we might find my parents too."

"Do you have any new leads?"

"Only Behemoth here. If he decides that we're telling the truth and that I'm a good person, then we'll be step closer to finding the book."

"How's that?"

I told Francis about our trip to the Natural History

Museum, how I'd picked up a Hell-goat, and Madaleine's murder.

"Ah shoot. This sounds like it's getting messy," she said.

"Yeah. And we still have no leads on Envy or Pride."

Francis blew out a sigh and stared at Behemoth. "Do you know anything that can help Beth?"

The goat blinked at her. "I'm not here to help."

"Rude."

He chittered. "I am not rude. I am a magnificent Hellbeast."

"You can still be rude."

"Francis," I interrupted her. "Please don't upset him. I need him to like me, remember?"

She folded her arms and gave the goat a pointed side-look. "Fine. On account of how magnificent you are, I'll retract the comment."

Behemoth jumped onto the bench beside her, and she jerked in surprise. "If you must know, I have been in the stone a while. I know little of use. I have opinions, but I am not supposed to share them."

"Why not?"

"They are for my mistress, and her alone." There was pride in his mental voice, and I jumped on the opportunity to soften up the little goat.

"She is very magnificent too," I said.

He nodded his golden horns. "And mighty."

"Does she know where the other sins are?"

"No," he said, then narrowed his eyes. "I was probably not supposed to say that."

Francis reached out and patted his head. He froze for a moment, the gold flecks in his fur lighting up with a weird glow. Francis froze too, a look of delighted fear on her face.

When she tentatively moved her hand again, Behemoth relaxed, and the glow faded. "I will allow you to touch me, but you should know that it is common courtesy to ask first."

Francis continued to stroke him, and he leaned in closer to her. "You got it," she said.

Rory and I sparred for nearly an hour before I ran out of energy. It felt good to concentrate my frustrations into something physical.

I was getting better too, catching Rory unawares on more blows than I had when we had started. I guessed the old adage that practice makes perfect was true. If I put in the hours every single day, I might actually end up able to defend myself. Well, at least from humans. A magic foe would still be beyond me.

The heat in my chest swelled, and I frowned. Was it reminding me it was there?

"Behemoth, what kind of magic will your stone amplify?"

"Any Hell magic," he answered sleepily. Francis was rubbing him under the chin now, and his eyes were half closed.

"What sort of magic is Hell magic?"

"There are all sorts, but the most common is fire."

"Rory, do you think I could use fire magic?"

She glanced at my wings, then shrugged. "Maybe. You'll have to ask Nox though. I don't have fire so I can't help you."

Claude was waiting for us in front of the retirement home. Francis made a small squeaking sound and stood up straighter as she walked. "There's that hunk of a driver," she whispered to me loudly.

I wouldn't describe Claude as a hunk, but for someone as old as he was, he was doing well. And he had kind eyes.

"Good day," he said to us as we reached him, tipping his cap.

"And a good day to you!" Francis exclaimed. Claude looked a little alarmed as she swooped toward him, kissing his cheek.

"I'll see you soon, Francis. Don't forget, if you see anything magical in the home, don't react," I said.

"Got it. Don't react."

Rory shook her head. "If you do, you'll get me fired."

Francis gave her an aghast look. "I wouldn't want that, not when you've been so kind to me. I swear, I'll do the best poker face you've ever seen, no matter what kind of magical beast I see."

"I don't think there are any magical beasts in the retirement home."

"That's what you think. I bet Ethel is a magical beast."

"Ethel is just mad."

"Nope. You wait. I'm gonna go back in there and she'll be covered in fur, and have wings, and-"

"Bye, Francis." Rory cut her off mid-rant, turning to walk toward the street, and Claude's car.

"Bye!" Francis waved enthusiastically after her.

"I'll see you soon," I told her, and Claude, Behemoth and I and followed the pixie.

Rory got in the front of the car with Claude, leaving me in the back with Behemoth.

"You know, you and Lucifer really are very interesting," the little goat said.

"Hmmm."

"I'm not in possession of all the facts. But I would like to be."

The more Behemoth talked, the more chance I had of learning something from him. Plus, I needed him to convince Techa I was a good person, which meant being honest with him. "Okay. What do you want to know?"

"This is what I am already sure of. Lucifer gave away the power of the sins that he did not want, which left him weaker. Now he wants them back, and somebody is trying to stop him, but you don't know who."

"Well, we know Banks is trying to stop him, but he's just a lunatic. We don't know who his behind the theft of his book. But your mistress does."

Behemoth shook his head. "No. She does not know who is behind it, only that a slimy shifter man sold it to her." He froze, realizing he'd said too much. Again. "Please, do not tell her I told you that."

I smiled at him. "My lips are sealed. That slimy shifter was called Max. He tried to kill me. Nox caught him, but whoever paid him to steal the book had put a tongue-tying curse on him. Want to tell me who Techa sold it on to?" I asked hopefully.

Behemoth let out his chirruping sound. "My life would not be worth living."

"So, how does a Hell-goat come to be the companion of a virtuous genie?"

"She bound me to my stone. I belong to her."

"Does that bother you?"

"No. Hell is strange place, and I was bored of it. Very few Hell creatures get to spend time freely in your world. And let me tell you, it's an excellent world."

"Yeah. It's pretty good." I let out a long sigh.

"This is the part I am missing," he said, his mental voice gentle. "Why does Lucifer want to return to Hell, when he clearly wants to be with you? You would not like Hell."

"Therein lies the problem," I muttered. "He is cursed. As long as he ignores his true role as punisher of sinners, he is deprived of... stuff. Important stuff."

The goat blinked at me. "What stuff?"

I closed my eyes. Nox would probably kill me for telling him. But we needed that book, and the best way to get it was convince Techa it was in everyone's best interest for Nox to get his power back. And to believe in his reasons for doing so. "Sex. We can't be together physically while he's cursed. Well, we can, but it will eventually kill him."

"Oh. That is unfortunate."

"Yeah."

"Could you be together and not have sex?"

"Maybe." *No.* He was freaking irresistible. "But even if we wanted to try that, Examinus has made it clear that he wants Nox to regain his power. Plus, someone is after him. And I want to find my parents, which might well be connected. Getting his power back and lifting the curse is really our only option. We'll have to work out the whole living-in-Hell thing later."

"Hmmm. I do not envy your situation. Although, it is exciting that you have found somebody that you feel so passionately about. Not all are so lucky."

"You know, that's true. I like your optimism." The sassy little Hell-goat was turning out to be good company.

"That angry lady in the museum was lucky too."

I snapped my eyes to him. "What?"

"She had found someone she felt passionately about. I am envious."

"How do you know that?"

"I could sense it."

"I think I could too," I said, feeling a slither of excitement. I didn't know if it was the Lust power sensing it, or just intuition, but I had been sure there was more going on with Cornu than she was letting on.

"The horned demon was a Hell creature, and I am very in tune with them, being that I'm from Hell too."

"You could tell how he felt?"

"I could tell he felt very proud of belonging to the angry angel."

"And her?"

"She was protective of him. She had Hell magic too, but she was very strong. It is much harder for me to read somebody that strong."

Protective. She might just have been protective because she wanted to keep her toy for herself. But could she have been protective because she loved him?

"Claude? Can we go to Shoreditch please?"

Rory leaned toward the hatch and looked at me. "What's at Shoreditch?"

"I think there was more to Madaleine and Cornu's relationship than she was letting on. And they never found him."

Rory raised one eyebrow. "You think he might know where the page is?"

"Maybe. If she really did trust him, he might know something."

She held my gaze a moment, then nodded. "It's worth pursuing. I'll let Nox know where we're going."

FOURTEEN

I only realized when I got to Madaleine's house that I didn't have magic door unlocking powers like the devil.

"Shit, Rory, can you get through locked doors?"

She gave me one of her 'duh' looks, and shiny pink swirls shot from her hand and zoomed into the keyhole of the black door at the top of the staircase.

"That's cool," I said. Rory didn't reply, but I was sure her face softened ever so slightly. The door clicked and we went in, Behemoth trotting along behind us. I headed straight up the stairs.

If I were in love with a guy and didn't want anyone to know, there would be two places I would hide my secret. First, on my phone. Second, under my pillow.

We didn't have her phone, so her pillow was my next best option.

The bedroom had a slightly staler scent to it than the day before, and I felt that uncomfortable sense of loss again. Madaleine had been so strong, such a force. Fear of whoever had been strong enough to brutally murder her shimmied through me, and I hurried toward the bed.

"Bingo."

There, under the pillow, was a small leather note-book. I sat on the edge of the bed just as Rory entered the room.

"Nice," she said, raising a brow as she looked around the dark room. "Did you find something?"

"Yeah, maybe."

Once again swallowing the sense that I was invading someone's privacy, I flipped open the book. It was full of photos. Photos and sketches. I turned the pages slowly, inspecting each picture.

Many were of places, and I wondered if it were a sort of travel journal. I recognized the Taj Mahal, the pyramids of Giza, the Colosseum in Rome. The earlier pictures in the book looked older, more faded. She appeared in a few of them, rarely smiling, always looking fierce and wearing white. As I carried on through the pages, I started to see a pattern. At first I'd thought they were just nonsense doodles, but I realized they all drew some inspiration from the architecture of whatever the photo was of. Some of the pictures were of food, and statues or artworks.

I turned a page and stopped. Cornu. Standing next to her. His smile, not predatory or wicked, but real. And so was hers. They were together at the top of the Empire State Building.

"He's here. In the book," I murmured. I kept flicking

through. There were four pictures of them together in London. And two of them were in the same place. "We need to go to the Ritz," I said.

There was a line to get into the restaurant when we arrived at the iconic London hotel nearly an hour later. I wasn't prepared for a crowd, and I was concentrating on filtering out the heightened sense of what everyone around me was feeling as we waited. The guy behind me was hungry, and the lady in front of me was having sexy thoughts about someone she wasn't supposed to.

"This is a nightmare," I mumbled, closing my eyes and rubbing my temples. "I don't know how Nox does it all the time." I opened my eyes and paused. Someone was standing at the corner of the building, wearing a beige overcoat and a scarf wrapped high around their face. My legs were moving before I could stop them. "Hold our place in the line," I called to Rory, and I ran toward where the figure had ducked out of view around the corner. By the time I skidded around the bend, I could see nobody in a coat that color. There were plenty of tourists and commuters, nearly all of them looking down at cellphones, but I could see nothing of the person I had chased.

"Damn it," I muttered.

"Who were you running after?"

I looked down at Behemoth. I hadn't realized he'd come with me. "I think someone is following us."

"Oh. In that case, I shall be on my guard. I am an excellent guard goat."

"Thanks, Behemoth."

I made my way back to the line for the Ritz, where Rory stood with her arms folded. "The overcoat thing again?" she asked.

"Yeah. Didn't catch them. Probably nothing." I tried to sound casual, but I was sure it *was* something now.

"Huh."

We stood in silence for another five minutes, and I wondered whether the person following me was a friend or foe. They could be Madaleine's murderer. If they'd wanted to hurt me, surely they would have by now? But then again, I'd never seen them when Nox was with me. Maybe they were waiting to hurt me, and just hadn't got me alone yet. A feeling of vulnerability began to seep into me, and the power in my chest flared. I needed to work on being able to defend myself, not think about being frightened.

"You're breathing hard." Nox's voice startled me, and I felt a burst of happiness as his familiar aura washed over me.

"Hi," I said, spinning around to see him. "Can you teach me to do fire magic?"

His mouth quirked up in a smile. "Is there a destructive side of you I've yet to see, Miss Abbott?"

"There's a side of me that doesn't want to get killed," I answered, and his playful look vanished. "In fact, all sides of me don't want to get killed."

"We'll try as soon as we can," he said.

"Excellent."

"So. You think Madaleine and Cornu were serious?" Nox asked me as the line shuffled forward.

"Yes."

"And you think you might find him here?"

"No, probably not right now. But I think we can leave him a message here. I left one at her house too."

"Saying what?"

"That I know he loved her and we want to avenge her death, and he should help us out."

Nox stared at me. "And you think that will work?"

"If he did love her, then yes. He will be grieving and angry. He will want to do anything he can to make the culprit pay, and you are his best shot at that."

Nox creased up his lovely face. "When you say it like that, it makes perfect sense. I would never have thought to just... ask."

"You'd have what, beaten it out of him?"

"Perhaps. He is a creature of Hell. I am his overlord. He must do as I bid him."

I shook my head. "Overlord? That sounds like something from a computer game."

"Call it what you like. I am the most powerful thing in Hell, besides a god. He belongs to me."

"Well, if I'm right, he's just lost the woman he loves. So maybe we could not be dicks about it?"

Nox's eyes hardened, light sparking in them. "I usually smite those who call me a dick," he said. "You test me, Miss Abbott."

I knew he was teasing, but he was giving off enough feral danger that my stomach turned somersaults.

"Smite away, Mr. Devil, Sir," I said, then regretted it instantly as images of him bending me over his knee, totally naked, filled my head.

I felt my face heating and swallowed.

I was saved from responding by the couple in front of us being ushered into the restaurant and the maître de smiling his greetings at us. He took one look at Nox, and the tips of his ears turned pink.

"Mr. Nox, sir, I am sorry to keep you waiting, I thought you knew that you could phone us to book ahead-"

Nox held his hand up and cut the guy off. "It's fine. Do you have a table for three?"

The maître de looked nervously down at his iPad. "For you, sir, of course. Give me a few moments."

He hurried off, returning barely sixty seconds later. "If you'll follow me, please."

The room we entered looked exactly like the photos in Madaleine's journal. It was easily recognizable to anyone who followed London magazines, like me. My love of food had led to years of treating the food critic sections akin to pornography.

A thrill of excitement took me as we were seated by the back wall, which was a grid of vintage mirrors. I'd always wanted to eat at the Ritz.

"Well, as we're here, what would you like?" Nox asked when the waiter handed us menus.

"We're supposed to be leaving Cornu a note," I protested, but it was half-assed.

I had written my note already, a carbon copy of the one I had left at Madaleine's house, and I looked around, trying to find somewhere I could put it that Cornu might find it if he came here. And I was sure he would. There were two photos of them together here, it must have been special to them in some way.

The problem was hiding it somewhere only he would find it - I didn't want anyone else to pick it up. "Nox, can you do something magic to the note so that only Cornu can see it?"

"No, but I can make it so that it's only visible to Hell creatures."

How many other demons would be passing through The Restaurant at the Ritz in the next few days? "I think that'll work."

I pulled some blue-tak out of my purse, and when I was sure nobody was looking, I leaned over and stuck the envelope with Cornu's name on the front to the mirrored wall. Nox waved his hand. Shadows whispered out of nowhere and swirled around the paper.

"Done," said Nox. "I'll ask the maître d' to let me know if any demons come by too."

"Is he magical?"

Nox gave me a look. "It's the Ritz. Of course there's magic here."

. . .

We had Afternoon Tea, but with champagne instead of tea. I smuggled food under the table for Behemoth, Rory actually smiled at one of my jokes, and for a blissful hour I got another glimpse of what life with Nox might be like if people didn't keep dying around us.

I wanted it, I realized, as I surreptitiously watched Nox. How anyone could look so damn graceful eating a scone, I didn't know. Knowing he couldn't taste it gave me a sour feeling in my gut though. He wasn't whole.

I would do anything for him to be happy. And that was something I'd never really felt before. Certainly not with the strength I was feeling it now.

I didn't want him to live in Hell or do the job he hated so much. But he couldn't live like this either. Cursed.

"You okay?" His voice was low as he looked at me, and I nodded. "You sure? You've gone quiet."

"Yes. Behemoth and Rory said the Saint thing might be a problem for you."

His expression tightened. "It's no more a problem than it was before. You can't live in Hell. That has not changed."

Anger bubbled through my chest, as it did every time I thought about not being with him.

His lips parted in a small smile. "I can feel you. My power inside you, reacting."

"Really?"

"Yes. The notion of us being apart angers you."

"Yes."

He leaned forward and kissed me. Nothing over the top. But it set every nerve in my body alight all the same.

"We'll see if you can use any of that power first thing tomorrow."

Excitement fired through me. "I can't wait."

"Good."

Nox's phone pinged, and he picked it up, scanning a message. "I need to go to the office."

"I have to go back to my place to sort some stuff out and pick up some clothes, but..." I trailed off, unsure how to broach the subject of where I should stay that night. I didn't want to assume he would want me in his spare room indefinitely, but it had kind of become the norm.

"Just call Claude when you're done and he'll pick you up and bring you to mine."

FIFTEEN

BETH

It took me a few hours to vacuum and clean my apartment and pack a new bag of clothes. I was fond of the place, but it sort of paled in comparison to Nox's. I patted the kitchen counter guiltily. It had been a lifeline for me when I came to England, and it felt oddly empty now.

Behemoth, who had followed me around the entire time I was cleaning, regaling me with tales of his mighty feats in Hell, chittered loudly as I scooped up my overnight bag. "My mistress calls," he said. "I assume she would like a report."

Nerves made my stomach flutter.

"I must return to the stone and entrust you to keep it safe and on your person until I am permitted to return and give you the verdict."

I swallowed. "Okay." I fished the egg-shaped stone out of my bag and it heated in my hands.

"Farewell for now," Behemoth said, then vanished

with a puff of dark purple light. The stone seared hot for a second, and I almost dropped it before it cooled.

Praying for a good outcome, I put the stone away and lifted my bag onto my shoulder. I was already looking forward to being back in the Grosvenor Road mansion.

The sun had dropped quickly, the shadows of the apartment blocks engulfing most of the light as I made my way down the fire escape stairs and turned toward the retirement home. I had a few DVDs in my bag to give to Francis, and I could sit with her while I waited for Claude. I was secretly keen to find out if there *were* any magical beasts in Lavender Oaks. Francis wasn't wrong - Ethel was a bit odd.

A faint smell caught my attention. Sulphur. I froze, sniffing hard. Hellhounds smelled like sulphur.

Surely I was just imagining it.

"Miss Abbott."

My heart slammed against my ribs, and I whirled at the voice.

"Banks?"

There was nobody there.

"You really fucked up my plan, you know that?"

"Where are you?"

Banks was powerful. I had no magic, and Rory and Nox weren't around. My pulse was racing, adrenaline causing sweat to prick my skin instantly.

I kept turning in a slow circle, eyes darting every-where, looking for any sign of movement.

Fire flickered at the edge of the nearest apartment building.

Sense forced its way through my panic, and I yanked my cellphone from the pocket of my leggings.

Before I could unlock it, it flew from my hands with a painful zap of electricity. Nox's power inside me responded to the magic, flaring to life.

Fight! Win!

The urge to stand up for myself, to punish this man who had tried to hurt Nox and kill me, filled me.

"Coward!" I yelled the word before I could help myself. The flickering around the edge of the brick building flared, and a huge beast stalked out of the shadows.

A Hellhound. Flaming and gnashing its jaws, it prowled toward me. A figure appeared behind it, illuminated by the fire.

Banks.

He was dressed in a long, black trenchcoat, and a dark scruff of facial hair made him look starkly different to the clean-cut officer of the law he had presented himself as when I had first met him.

"Where's the Warden you kidnapped?" I stood my ground, trying to glare at Banks instead of the flaming hound moving closer to me by the second.

"Cheryl? Don't you worry about Cheryl." He shrugged.

"How are you controlling the Hellhounds?"

"Why the fuck would I tell you that? I'm here because you have something I want."

I scowled. "I have nothing."

"Not true. You have Nox."

"Why do you want Nox?" Fear was crawling up my spine as the heat from the Hellhound licked at my skin, but rather than immobilize me, the fear moved my feet.

I backed away, aware that I was moving farther from my apartment but not being given much choice.

Banks followed the hound, firelight making the shadows on his face move menacingly. "My business is not yours. Now, if you'll come with me, you can find out first-hand how Cheryl is."

The Hellhound snarled and dropped its shoulders. A slow smile spread across Banks' face.

My mind raced, desperate for a way out. I had no cellphone. Nox wasn't here. Would anyone hear me if I screamed? It might attract the attention of the other residents, but would that help? What if someone else got hurt because of me? It was unlikely that I shared a residential estate with anyone able to fight off a Hellhound.

The beast pounced.

I threw myself to the side and launched into a sprint. I didn't even look which direction I was going, just powered my legs as fast as they would move. But the creature was huge, its stride easily outpacing mine. Heat seared up my back and I banked sharply between two apartment blocks. There was a slight squeal and a thud, but I didn't stop to see what had happened.

Maybe if I could get to the main road, where there were simply too many cars and people for Banks and the Hellhound to ignore, I would be safe. I ran on, praying that by some miracle I could outpace the beast.

A loud laugh filled my ears and an explosion of light sent me skidding to a stop. Banks stepped out of the sparking air in front of me while I blinked in panic.

Spinning, I saw the Hellhound behind me. I was trapped.

"Nox will find me, and he'll deliver on his promise," I growled. "He'll tear you limb from limb."

A cruel glint shone in Banks' eyes. He opened his mouth to speak, but then his expression changed, shock morphing his features. His eyes glazed over, and he crumpled to the ground. There was a snarling noise behind me and I turned to see a fizz of green light, then the Hellhound collapsed to the ground too.

"We've got seconds before they come around. You need to get somewhere safe," a woman's voice said, before she emerged from the shadows of the nearest building. She was wearing a beige overcoat and holding a small crossbow that glowed green.

Every muscle in my body froze as my stomach swooped.

"Mom."

SIXTEEN

BETH

"Somewhere safe, Bethany. Now."

But my brain was stuck. My eyes raced over her face repeatedly in the gloom, taking in every single detail.

For years, I thought she was dead. I'd mourned her loss. And then hope had given me the faintest belief I might see her again.

"You're here." My words were a whisper. "You're alive."

"Neither of us will be for much longer when they wake up." Her stern tone sent roiling emotions crashing through me, years of memories flooding my mind.

"How? How are you here?"

"Bethany, we need to get somewhere safe, now!" She grabbed my arm as she raised her voice, and my daze lifted enough to register the flaming dog on the ground before us.

"The road. Do you have a phone?"

"No."

"We'll flag a cab."

I gripped her hand, a weird pulse of energy rippling through me, then tugged her along the path. She broke into a jog beside me, then a run.

There were scores of taxis on any road in in London at any given moment, and mercifully we barely had to stop when we reached the sidewalk to wave one down. We both looked frantically over our shoulders as we dove into the car, and when I asked the driver to get us to Grosvenor Street as fast as he could, he rolled his eyes at me.

"This ain't some movie, love," he grumbled, pulling out slowly into the traffic. I stared out of the window as a flicker of orange shone beyond the buildings that made up my estate.

"I'll pay double if you can get us there in twenty minutes."

"What? It's a forty-minute trip." He frowned at me in the mirror.

"Double," I repeated. "If you can do it in half the time."

He gave me a long look and then the car lurched forward.

I turned in my seat, staring at the woman before me, my mind tumbling through question after question, unable to choose the right one.

My mom.

She hadn't aged a day. Her blonde hair was neatly secured in a bun—her thin lips and clear blue eyes were just as I remembered them. She was wearing black slacks and the beige overcoat. She was looking back at me with the same expression she'd worn my entire childhood, and the portion of my adulthood that she'd been around. One of stern patience.

"Where have you been?" My voice cracked. I saw the slightest flicker of something in her eyes, and she let out a long breath. "Why have you been following me, hiding from me?"

"You're not going to like the answers, Beth."

Anger flashed through me. "You think I enjoyed believing you were both dead? Where's dad?"

This time I was sure I could see pain in her expression. "I can't tell you."

I gaped at her. "What?"

"I can't tell you. I know it sounds unlikely, but I truly can't."

"This is not happening," I breathed deeply, rubbing my hands across my face, aware of how close I was to tipping to the wrong side of control. Overwhelmed didn't come close to how I was feeling. "Mom, you have just shown up to save me from a damn Hellhound after disappearing for five years. Tell me where dad is, and what the hell is going on!"

"There's no need for swearing," she said, lips pursed.

"Are you freaking kidding? If there was ever a time for swearing it's now!" My voice had risen enough that the cab driver glanced over his shoulder at us.

"Beth, calm down."

"No! Why did you leave me?" My eyes burned, and my tenuous control abandoned me. "Is dad alive?"

"Yes."

I gulped down air as my tears fell.

Thank god. Thank god he was alive. *They were both alive.*

Relief finally overwhelmed me, breaking through the panicked shock. Years of grief and dashed hope amassed in one epic tidal wave of emotion, and a sob broke free from my throat. Mom reached out awkwardly. She had never, ever, been comfortable with affection. But at that moment, I didn't care. I threw my arms around her and let the tears come.

"I missed you," I snuffled into her shoulder as she patted my head. "I missed you both so much. I looked for you, for years. I thought you were dead."

"I'm so sorry, Beth."

I leaned back, wiping my face with my arm. "Where were you? Why did you leave?"

"Honestly, Beth, I can't tell you. I wish I could."

"Why? Why can't you tell me?"

She stared at me, her stern face giving me nothing. "I didn't want to leave."

"You were kidnapped?"

"Yes."

"By who? The same person trying to take down Nox?"

He mouth tightened even more. "I can't begin to tell you how disappointed I am in the company you have chosen to keep, Bethany. I assume that's where you are going now? To visit with the devil?"

She said devil as though the word was filthy.

"Mom, who took you and dad?"

"If you keep asking me the same questions, then I'll be forced to keep repeating myself. I can't tell you."

"Can't or won't?"

She sighed again. "I knew this would be hard. As you are so insistent, I will prove it to you." Her voice thickened as her sentence ended and she took a massive breath. "The kidnapper-"

She fell forward suddenly. "Mom?"

Her head tipped back, her skin white, and her little crossbow clattered to the seat as she clutched at her throat.

Bile rose in my own throat as I saw what was happening. Her tongue was splitting as I watched, turning into a writhing mass of tiny snake-like things, filling her mouth. Heat billowed from my chest unbidden, wrapping around us both and the awful snake-tongues slowed. "Mom," I said again, gripping her arm, no idea how to help her.

All I could do was watch her try to suck in air until the snakes shrank down, and her tongue finally pieced itself back together.

"Now do you believe me?" she choked when she

could speak again. "I have a tongue-tying curse. Everyone they have taken has the same treatment."

I remembered what had happened to Max's tongue whenever he had been questioned and I shuddered, rubbing her back. She'd spent five years captive to a monster. "How did you escape? Wait, were you a captive at Ward HQ? Why did you say what you said on the radio about me not finding you?"

She stiffened suddenly, and the crossbow beside her flared with light. "I shouldn't have helped you," she hissed. "I must go, now."

"No!" I gripped her arm tightly, panic flooding me. "No, I've just found you, you can't go!"

"I must."

"Was the note from you?" I hesitated, unable to get the next question out. *Did you kill Madaleine?*

"Do not speak of these things, Bethany. I must go."

"Please, Mom. At least... At least tell me if dad's okay? Does he miss me?" I knew I sounded like a wounded child, but I didn't care.

Mom's eyes softened, her sternness falling away as she squeezed my hand. "He would be here in my place in a heartbeat. He has missed you every day. As have I."

Fresh tears ran down my cheeks. "I have so many questions," I said, trying to get my thoughts into any kind of useful order.

"I'm sorry, Beth," she said. "Keep your father's Hope alive." A burst of green light engulfed her, and she vanished.

SEVENTEEN

BETH

By the time we approached Nox's house on Grosvenor Street, I had slipped into some sort of stupefied daze. My tears had stopped, but a sort of numbness had taken me. The driver hadn't made it in twenty minutes, but he scraped just under thirty. I paid him the extra, then jogged up the steps to the front door. My legs were leaden, the showdown with Banks starting to take its toll. Adrenaline was still coursing through me, making my hands shake as I grabbed the knocker. It didn't even occur to me to use my new key.

The door opened.

"Nox-" I began, but his face darkened, and he stepped toward me, sweeping me into his arms.

"That's... Sulphur." He tensed, and heat surged from him. "What happened?"

"Banks. With his own pet Hellhound." Nox pushed me back to look into my face. Hot anger poured from his body. "And... My Mom saved me. She knocked Banks and the Hellhound out with some sort of green magic, and now... Now she's gone again."

I saw his eyes widen, then soften. "Come inside."

Nox led us to a room I hadn't been in before, at the back of the ground floor of the house. It was a sitting room with two large white leather couches, and a big shagpile rug in the middle of the room. Tall art deco lamps stood in each corner, and a huge fireplace with a marble mantle dominated the back wall. The firewood in the hearth was unlit.

He sat me down on the couch, then crouched in front of me and locked his eyes on my face. His heat had lessened, but his expression was still severe. He gripped my hand in his, and that delicious blanket of warmth engulfed me. My mind cleared a little, and air seemed to flow into my lungs better. "Tell me what happened."

"Banks was waiting outside my apartment. He said he wanted to take me, to get to you. He and the Hellhound had me trapped, and then my mom shot him and the hound with a green crossbow and knocked them out." I blinked up at him. "My Mom, Nox. My Mom."

Tears filled my eyes again, hot, and my throat quivered. But now that I was with Nox, his heat and his safety wrapping me up, my mind was clear enough to wade through the overwhelming emotions, and land on one realization.

I threw my arms around Nox, letting the tears come. "Nox, they're alive! They're both alive. Dad's an angel of Hope, and he's alive."

I leaned back, and Nox's smile made my chest swell

even more as a laugh escaped me. It was a true smile, and his relief was clear in his bright eyes.

"I can't believe it. I saw her. I saw my mom, and they're both alive."

"Tell me what she said to you."

I did my best to recount the conversation as accurately as I could. Nox's smile slowly slipped away as I spoke.

"Beth... This all plays into your theory about the Saints being kidnapped. Whoever is behind this is powerful and dangerous. And it doesn't sound like your mom escaped them."

"What?"

"Your Mom is human. For a human to use a weapon like that, it must be imbued with magic by someone else."

I stared at him, trying to work out what he was saying. "So, someone gave her a magic weapon?"

"Yes."

"The person who helped her escape?"

"Or her captor."

"I don't understand."

"She's been following you but keeping her distance. Why would she do that? You're her daughter - she should have come straight to you as soon as she found you. You heard her say on the radio that she didn't want you to find her. Someone summoned her away before she could say too much to you in the car just now. None of this sounds good." His voice was gentle but felt like knives in my skull.

He was right.

Mom's awkward lack of affection was characteristic, but she loved me and always had. Surely if she had escaped the tongue-tying monster who had held her captive, she would have sought me out straight away, not hidden from me in the shadows.

"But she's helping me. The note about the museum, and saving me from Banks..."

"I don't believe she escaped, Beth. I think she's been sent to London. Probably by her captor."

"Why?"

"She can use you to get to me."

"What? No." I shook my head, confused. "No. She's my Mom."

"Which is why she broke the rules and saved you from Banks today. But Beth, she must have some purpose here, and she is being backed by someone with strong magic. It is not easy to knock out a Hellhound or an angel."

"My Mom is a good person. The *best* person, she's virtuous and selfless and kind. She wouldn't be dishonest or do the bidding of a kidnapper, or a murderer, ever."

Nox squeezed my hand hard. "What would she do to save your father?"

I stared at him. What *would* she do?

"I'm not suggesting that she is a bad person, or that she doesn't love you. But we need to be very, very careful here. She is the perfect trap."

Anger mingled with my confusion, and I pulled my hand from his. "Trap? She's not a trap, she's my mother. She just saved my life."

"And I am eternally grateful to her for that," he breathed. "Beth, I pledge to you now that I will do anything in my power to save her and your father. Anything."

His wings slowly unfurled behind him, and a bright golden glow lit the room as they extended wide, the feathers gleaming.

"What are you doing?"

"Making a vow. I may be a fallen angel, but I'm an angel all the same. My vow is unbreakable."

He reached his hands out again, and after a second's hesitation, I took them.

Sparks fired at the contact, and a rush of power hit me, an overwhelming sense of conviction assaulting my senses. True, unbridled commitment poured from him, into me.

He would keep his word. He would do anything he could to save my parents.

He wouldn't stop until they were safe. He was with me in this until the end, whatever happened.

I was no longer alone.

"Thank you," I whispered. The glow from his wings behind him was so bright that his face appeared darker, save for his intensely bright blue eyes. I reached out, running my fingers along the hard plane of his jaw, so strong against the soft golden feathers. He was breath-taking, kneeling before me. Divine.

"I would do anything for you, Beth."

"And I you."

And I knew it was true. For both of us.

I drew in air, trying to focus. I longed to throw myself into him, forget everything. But I had just seen my mom. For the first time in five years.

And what Nox had said was undeniable. Something wasn't right.

"Nox, I don't know what to do," I breathed.

"Have a drink, I think." He stood, running his thumb along my cheek as he did. He wings slowly curled back into his back, their glow dimming. He was wearing jeans and fitted t-shirt, and I realized with a vague detachment that he was barefoot.

He moved to a wooden globe on wheels and lifted the top to reveal a bar inside. I watched him pour amber liquid into two tumblers.

I replayed his words, processing their sense.

Mom didn't escape. She herself never said she escaped. So, what was her plan? Who was giving her the magic?

"Here." Nox handed me one of the tumblers. Scotch, I realized as the scent hit me.

I knocked back a big gulp gratefully, relishing the burn as it moved through my throat.

"Mom can't be associated with Banks, given that she shot him. Banks made it clear that he's after you," I said. "Why?"

Nox eased onto the sofa beside me. "I don't know. All I know is that I will kill him."

The lethal venom in his tone made me flinch. Part of me recoiled at the notion of him killing someone. The other part of me recalled Banks' face when he'd tried to kill me in the cell, and the primal terror the Hellhounds instilled in me. That part of me wanted Nox to make sure Banks could never harm anyone again.

"I think he killed Madaleine. For her page," I said.

Nox raised an eyebrow. "I hate to ask you this, but is there any chance it could have been your mom?"

I shook my head. "No. She might have been there, or know who did, but I don't believe she could kill someone."

"Perhaps not directly. But could she have lured Madaleine there? For whoever it is who's given her the magic?"

I shifted uncomfortably, then took another swig of the whiskey. "No." I changed the subject. "What kind of magic could make her disappear in a puff of light like she did? Your brothers do that, don't they? But I've never seen you do it."

"I can move around like that in Hell, but not here, in your world. Technically, I do not belong here, like my brothers do." He ground out the last sentence. "It is an uncommon magic, for sure. Even more so to do it to someone else. Genies could do it."

"Could Techa be behind this?"

Nox frowned. "She is as virtuous as it sounds like your mother is."

"Maybe they are helping each other?"

Nox shook his head. "Unlikely."

I sighed. "Do you think I'll see her again?"

"Yes."

"Soon?"

"Yes."

"I can't tell you how relieved I am that they're both alive. Whatever her purpose is, she saved me today. I've spent years dreaming of seeing her face again. And today, I did." I took another deep drink.

"We will find them. And in the meantime, hopefully Behemoth is telling Techa everything she needs to hear, and we will find out who has the book."

"What if he doesn't?"

Nox took a long sip of his own drink before looking at me. "Then I'll tear London apart myself to find it."

EIGHTEEN

"Good morning, gorgeous."

The sultry Irish accent dragged me from a deep sleep, and I rolled over, blinking my grogginess away. Nox was standing next to the guest room bed.

"Hi."

He reached out, stroking loose hair from my face. I had a moment of panic that he was seeing me with no make-up on, and my hair a mess, but when he leaned down and kissed my forehead, my panic vanished. "How are you feeling?"

I took a second to work out my answer before I gave it to him. "Happy. The best news I could possibly have hoped for was that they were both alive. And they are. Even better, my mom's looking out for me. She saved me yesterday."

Plus, I wasn't alone in my quest to find them anymore. Nox had made an unbreakable vow to see this though with me, whatever happened. Hy heart seemed to swell in my chest as I gazed up at him.

He smiled. "Get dressed. We've got a lot to do today. We need to make sure you don't need someone else to save you."

"Huh?"

"Malcolm has finally got his hands on something. Something for you. We need to go pick it up and tell him what we now know about your mom."

"What is it?"

"A weapon. And then we need to see if you can use any of that lovely Hell magic inside of you."

Excitement had me sitting up straight in a heartbeat.

"I'm really going to try to learn magic?"

"Yup. I'll see you downstairs."

I got dressed lightning-fast, opting for casual stretch jeans and a T-shirt, so that I could move easily if I needed to.

Claude was outside the house, and he handed us both ceramic travel mugs before opening the car doors for us. "Thanks, Claude."

I sniffed, the delicious scent of coffee filling my nose as I settled into the leather seat. "I love this car," I said. "I always feel safe in this car."

Nox reached over and settled his hand on my knee. "You can always feel safe with me."

"I'll feel even safer if I've got a magical weapon," I said, sounding a little like a kid at Christmas.

"Good morning!" There was a puff of black and purple light, and Behemoth appeared on the seat opposite me. "I am back," the little goat announced, entirely unnecessarily.

My stomach lurched. "So I see. Did you talk to Techa?"

"I did."

I raised my eyebrows, waiting for more. But Behemoth just stared back at me. "What did she say?"

"That she can't see any reason to help you."

My stomach sank.

"Then why are you back here?" Nox ground out.

"Because you want your stone back, I imagine," I sighed, moving to get it from my purse.

"No. I am back because I am convinced that you are worth more time. It has not been long enough to give a good report. I was able to make my mistress see my point, and she has permitted me to continue my observations."

Hope buoyed me. *Hope. My father's power.* I beamed at Behemoth, leaned forward, and patted him between the horns. "You're right, Behemoth. It hasn't been enough time. Thank you."

He nodded his head. "Indeed. Did I miss anything while I was gone?"

"Erm, yeah. Just a little."

~

~

When Nox knocked on Malc's office door, I found myself oddly glad to see the vampire's pale face.

"Boss, Lady Boss," he said with a grin as we entered the dark room.

"About this Lady Boss thing, I'm not your boss-" I started to say, but Malc waved his hands enthusiastically in the air, shaking his head.

"Too late! It's stuck now, I can't possibly call you anything else. Plus, you're banging the boss. Makes you Lady Boss."

I sighed.

"Is that a Hell-goat?" Malc said, staring down at Behemoth.

"Yes. Where's this weapon?" Nox said.

"Cool," said Malc, peering down at the goat, who was now preening slightly.

"I am not cool, I am hot. And fierce," Behemoth said.

Malc grinned. "You sure are."

"Malcolm. The crossbow. Now."

"Sorry Boss." Malc got up from his chair, a thing I realized I'd never seen him do, and sauntered around the desk.

"You are way taller than I realized you were," I said.

"Six foot nine," he muttered, ducking down. "Here we go." He straightened, and in his hand was a small crossbow.

"But... But that's just like the one my mom had."

Malc blinked at me, his red eyes shining. "Probably,

yeah. Your Mom is human. These are like, one of two magical weapons a human can use. The other is a mace and there are only three in the whole world, so I'd be mega impressed if she had one of those." His face crumpled into a frown. "Wait, did you see your mom?"

"I did." I told him what had happened, and he was back at his desk before I had finished, fingers flying over the keys of keyboard.

"Tongue tying magic is foul," he said when I'd finished. "Filthy magic."

"It was horrible to watch."

"So, she was the one following you in the overcoat?"

"How'd you know about that?"

"Rory told me each time you saw them."

"She did?"

"Yup." He picked up the crossbow from where he'd put it on the table. "These don't normally glow green and they shouldn't be able to take out Hellhounds."

Nox spoke, his voice deep in contrast to Malc's excitable chatter. "This one will be effective against Hellhounds because it will be imbued with my magic."

I nodded, both excited at having something to use against the horrifying creatures, and praying that I would never need to.

"But Malcolm is right, it is surprising that the one your Mom had worked."

"I wonder who imbued hers with magic?" Malc mused aloud. "We heard her talking to someone at Ward HQ. They could be helping her," he suggested.

"They could also be her captors," Nox snarled.

"I can't see Michael abducting angels, Boss," said Malc, awkwardly.

"This discussion is over," Nox said, and Malc whirled back to his monitor.

"I'm looking up green magic, and I'll check CCTV footage from where you saw her near the Ritz. I'll also recheck what I got from the museum. We might be able to see where she goes when she stops following you, Beth."

"Good," Nox said as he yanked the door open. Malc pushed the crossbow along the desk toward me, averting his eyes from the dim light from the open door.

"Good luck," he whispered.

"Thanks," I said, swiping up the weapon and hurrying after Nox.

"Where are we going to learn to use this?" I asked, turning the little weapon over in my lap once we were back in the car. It was lightweight, the body of it made of a dark resin, and the little bow shape at the front and the trigger underneath a shiny bronze material. There was a slender metal bolt loaded in the groove at the top that didn't seem to fall out, even when I turned it upside down. It was light enough that I guessed it could easily be fired with one hand.

"My place," Nox answered. He reached over, touching the crossbow. "It only has one bolt, which doesn't actually leave the weapon. The bolt channels magic, and fires that in its place."

"Okay."

"Have you fired a crossbow before?"

"No. But I learned to fire a handgun before I came to London."

He raised one eyebrow. "Good. Then you know about recoil and kickback." I nodded. "This is the same, so aim low. And to ready it, you pull back this wire." He touched the tight wire joining the bow at the front to the barrel.

"Got it."

We fell silent a few moments.

"Nox, where in your house are we practicing? Because I don't want to mess up any of your fancy stuff."

He gave me a dark smile. "There's plenty of my house you haven't seen, Miss Abbott."

"How have you managed to make that sound so dirty? Like you have a secret sex dungeon Madaleine would be proud of or something," I muttered.

"I don't have a secret sex dungeon. But if you wanted me to, I would happily install one."

We did head down to the basement when we got back to Grosvenor Street, but it was not to a dungeon. It was to a well-lit, modern gymnasium, with an archery range dominating the back wall.

"You have a gym?" I asked as I entered.

"I have a gym, yes. I also have a sauna, a hot tub, a pool, a movie theatre, a library, and a wine cellar."

"Huh."

The room was paneled in pale wood that made it feel distinctly masculine, and oddly cozy for a gym. It had all the usual equipment I would expect to see, like treadmills and weight benches, along with a smell of refrigerated air about it.

Nox made his way over to the archery range and I followed him.

"We need to imbue the crossbow with magic," he said, and I held the weapon up so he could take it. He shook his head.

"I thought we were putting your magic in it?" I frowned.

"I want to see if you can channel the magic inside you into the weapon."

I stared down doubtfully at the weapon. "I can try."

"Get Behemoth's stone. It should help."

"Okay." I got the stone from my purse, slipping the bag from my shoulder and setting it down on the floor. I looked at Nox, stone in one hand, crossbow in the other.

"Just do exactly as I tell you. Close your eyes."

Doing exactly as Nox told me had worked out very well for me so far, so I dutifully shut my eyes.

"Good. Now, feel for my magic inside you. Where is it?"

I touched one hand to my chest. "Here."

"Embrace it. Let it burn."

I did as he said, willing the feeling that was becoming familiar now to rise within me.

I could feel it, but only a little.

"It usually only comes when you're not there," I told Nox. "Like it's making up for your absence or something."

"What else causes you to feel it?"

"People suggesting we can't be together," I admitted.

There was a pause, but just before I was about to open my eyes, he spoke again. "Think about that. If you feel the magic inside you, try to direct it into the weapon. See the weapon as an extension of yourself. Something to defend you against those who would harm you. Or... Or something to use against those who would keep us apart."

I did as he said.

I thought about what Behemoth, Rory, and Madaleine had said about us being a bad match. A fallen angel and a human girl, kept apart by a lethal curse and an enemy in the shadows.

The heat built in my chest. The voice in my mind, my own but so much fiercer, began to speak.

He's mine. We have to be together. We will be together. And fuck anybody who tries to stop us. I will take them down.

The crossbow seared my hand, and my eyes flew open. Gold light pulsed from it, shadows swirled over the wire, and coiled around the barrel.

I looked up at Nox, who had a dark smile on his face.

"Congratulations. You have a Hell-magic powered crossbow."

"I do?"

"You do. Also, your wings are fucking beautiful."

He pointed to a full-length mirror on the other side of the gym, and I gasped.

He wasn't wrong. My tiny translucent wings were no longer tiny and translucent. They weren't anything on Nox's, but they were solid. I walked slowly toward the mirror, gaping. The feathers were lighter than Nox's, and less bright, and there were a lot less shadows moving over them. I willed them to move, experimentally, trying to feel internally for my shoulder blades.

I felt cool air skim my back, and the wings in my reflection rustled.

"Oh my god," I breathed. "I moved them!"

Nox chuckled. "Imagine filling a space with them. Picture it, then flex your shoulders."

I did, and slowly, my wings extended, stretching out. An *ooh* escaped my mouth. I'd pretty much forgotten about the glowing crossbow in my hand. I whirled to face Nox. "Can I fly?"

His face turned serious. "Very few winged creatures can actually fly and its extremely dangerous to try."

My shoulders slumped a little. "That's a no then."

"You don't need to be able to fly. You have me."

Nox's own wings burst out behind him, and my smile returned. I stepped toward him, and his feathers fluttered.

A ringing sound made me pause, and Nox frowned before pulling his cellphone from his pocket.

"Only Rory's calls are coming through right now, and

she knows I'm not to be disturbed today. If she's phoning, then it's important," he said, apologetically.

I nodded, and he lifted the phone to his ear. "Yes?" he barked into the receiver. I watched the annoyance fall from his face. He looked at me. "The Ritz have just called. I think they've found your demon."

NINETEEN

BETH

Nox said it was quicker to walk to the Ritz than drive, and he was right. Our brisk pace got us there in just eight minutes.

"You can't come in, sir," a security guard was saying, standing on the sidewalk and trying to block the entrance to the restaurant. In front of him, disheveled and swaying slightly, was Cornu.

I stepped toward him, moving slowly, not wanting to draw the attention of the demon yet. But Nox stepped up behind me, and Cornu's eyes flashed up to us immediately, his slurred protests to the security guard halting. I saw him tense, and knew he was about to run.

A wave of heat pulsed from behind me, and Cornu gave a small grunt. Shadowy tendrils wrapped around him, holding him still. The security guard was frowning.

"Are you alright? Do you have pain?"

I realized that if you couldn't see the shadows, it looked a lot like Cornu was seizing or having a heart attack or something. I moved over to him quickly, and the smell of whisky rolling off Cornu hit me as soon as I got close.

"He's fine," I told the guard, putting my hand on Cornu's arm. His skin was hot and damp under his thin shirt, and he grunted. "Just had a little too much to drink. We'll take it from here."

The guard opened his mouth, clearly concerned, but when he saw Nox behind me, he nodded.

The shadows flared and Cornu turned awkwardly, as though he was a reluctant puppet. Together, we made our way down the street. At the end of the block, we reached Green Park, and I headed straight for a large vacant bench. The shadows vanished and Cornu slumped down onto it.

"What the fuck do you want?" he snarled. His eyes were red-ringed and sunken, and his clothes were clearly not fresh.

"I'm sorry about Madaleine," I said, sitting next to him.

"Bullshit." He glared up at Nox. "You were going to take her power away from her."

Nox started to speak, and I jumped up from the bench. "Give me a few minutes. Please."

Nox eyed me a second, then looked at the demon. "Try to run, and it will hurt," he said.

Cornu made an angry sound in his throat and glared at the ground, refusing to look at Nox. It was a show of defiance, and I could feel Nox getting angry. "Please," I said again, glaring at him.

Nox whirled, stamping off toward a large oak tree. Behemoth stayed right where he was, at my ankles. I sat back down on the bench.

"I know she loved you," I said quietly. Cornu's snapped his eyes to mine.

"How?"

"I saw it in her face and heard it in her voice."

He shook his head. "She didn't want anyone to know. I'm just a demon, and she..." He took a shuddering breath. "She was a fucking goddess amongst angels. She was incredible."

"I admired her. She was a lot of things I would love to be."

Cornu looked into my face, his eyes gleaming with unshed tears. "You could never be her. Nobody could."

"I know. Let me help you avenge her."

He eyes narrowed, distrust clouding his expression. "Lucifer wanted to fuck up her life. I don't know why she was helping him."

So she *was* trying to help? That was interesting. "Did she write me a note to go to the museum?"

Cornu shrugged. "We went there because she heard the book of sins might have passed through. I wish we fucking hadn't."

"What happened?" I asked as gently as I could, but he tensed up beside me.

"I don't know. I was sent back to Hell."

"By Madaleine?"

"No. She would never do that. I was just walking next to her, past the trinity painting, and then boom, I was in Hell. It took me over an hour to get back, and when I did…"

"Do you have any idea who it was? Or why?"

"Lucifer and his stupid fucking book. That's why we were in the museum. It's his fault." He glared over at where Nox and Rory were talking under the tree.

"Someone is trying to kill him too. We want to stop them. I think it's the same person. We have the same enemy, Cornu."

He fell silent a moment, then spoke quietly. "What do you want from me? I have to do whatever that prick Lucifer wants me to do, and without Madaleine, what's the fucking point in fighting?"

"Madaleine didn't sell her sin page, did she?" Cornu leaned forward, his elbows on his thighs, and put his head in his hands. His horns protruded from either side as he scrubbed his fingers angrily through his hair.

"It was hers. These are her secrets, they don't belong to you."

"I'm sorry, Cornu. I am. But this is the only way we can make sure Madaleine's killer is caught."

He looked sideways at me. "Will they suffer?"

I swallowed uncomfortably. I didn't like the notion of anyone suffering. But if we caught whoever was behind this, there was little chance that Nox would take it easy. And if it turned out to be Banks, I might even shift my position on people suffering. That man deserved a beating.

"Nox is known for his punishments," I said, slightly evasively.

"I want to be there."

I sucked in a breath. "I can't make that happen. We don't even know who it is-"

"I want to be there," he repeated. "If you promise I can be there when Nox punishes her killer, I'll give you the page."

My pulse quickened, and I felt my body stiffen in anticipation. "You know where it is?"

He nodded.

I bit my lip as I thought. Nox could just make him hand it over. By telling me that he knew where it was, he'd given his hand away. And wanting to watch a person be punished by the devil was pretty macabre. But Cornu was a demon, a creature born from Hell, and that was his world. The woman he loved had just been murdered.

I looked into his desperate face and found myself speaking. "Okay. I promise I'll do whatever I can. *If* we catch whoever it is." I emphasized 'if'.

"You swear? You'll make Lucifer let me be there?"

"I can't *make* Nox do anything, but I'll try my best."

Cornu got slowly to his feet and wobbled slightly. "Call Lucifer."

TWENTY

BETH

"Cornu is going to take us to the page," I said as I reached Nox by the tree. The demon gave Nox an angry look as he swayed from foot to foot over at the bench.

"He knows where it is?"

"Yes."

"And he's giving it to us voluntarily?" I could hear the doubt in Nox's tone, and I could see why. The demon's hatred for him was pouring from every pore.

"Sort of," I said awkwardly, refusing to catch his eye. "I'll tell you later."

Nox opened his mouth, considered me a moment, then closed it again. "Lead on."

Together, we walked to Cornu. "I have a car nearby," Nox said. "Where are we going?"

"No need." He lifted his hand and hit himself hard in the chest. "I'm the hiding place. She hid the page in me."

I between Nox and Cornu. "What does that mean? Because it sounds unpleasant."

"Madaleine was chosen to host Wrath for a good reason. She was one of the most powerful fallen angels I knew, and not afraid of anything. Including some pretty nasty Hell magic," said Nox quietly. He fixed his gaze on Cornu. "She bound the page to you?"

He shook his head. "No. To my home, in Hell. I'm the key."

"How does that work?" I asked.

Nox looked at me. "Madaleine hid the page in Hell, and made sure it could only be accessed through Cornu. She was smart. Only a very powerful being from Hell could force the page from him."

"A very powerful being from Hell, like you," Cornu spat. "There was nowhere she could hide it that you couldn't access."

"This doesn't have to hurt," Nox said to the demon. "If you co-operate."

Cornu sneered at him. "There is nothing that could fucking hurt me now. Not now."

Nox stilled. "Let's get this over with," he said. "What incantation did she use?"

The air behind Cornu shimmered, and flashes of black and deep, burning red swirled in and out of existence as Nox chanted alien words I assumed were Latin. Behemoth chittered excitedly next to me, Cornu's horns seared a scarlet color, and his face crumpled in pain. My instinct was to step in, to do something to help, but Behemoth barked into my mind.

"Lucifer knows what he's doing."

"Is that Hell behind Cornu?"

"Yes."

I watched as Nox raised his arms, golden wings spread wide and shadows turning in tornados around him. I looked around the park. Folk were sitting on the grass, eating, or reading books. A couple were walking a white, fluffy dog down a path. Nobody could see the freaking angel of Hell standing in their midst.

Suddenly, all the shadowy tornados rushed Cornu, and he vanished.

"Is that supposed to happen?"

Rory didn't answer me.

Nox stayed exactly where he was, heat radiating from him, eyes closed. With a crack of thunder so loud it made me gasp, Cornu reappeared, tumbling to the ground in a flash of red and black. He rolled onto his hands and knees and vomited on the ground.

"Oh my god, are you okay?"

He rocked back onto his heels as I approached. He reeked of sulphur, and sweat was pouring down his face and neck. His horns were pulsing a weird dark matter.

"Here." He thrust out his hand, a small piece of paper rolled up in it. "Keep your promise. Please." I looked into his pale, exhausted face as I took the little scroll from him.

"I will."

. . .

As soon as Nox took the piece of paper from me, shadows began flying from the little page as though they were being sucked out, and then whipped up by an invisible wind.

He clapped his hands together, and when he drew them apart blue light burned bright between his palms. The shadows dove into the light, spinning like a tornado, and after a beat, I saw them rushing over his gleaming feathers, swirling and ethereal.

I let out a long breath as the light faded away.

We'd done it. We'd found one more lost sin.

Nox was quiet until we got back to the car and we were alone. Well, sort of alone. If you didn't count Behemoth.

"What did you promise Cornu?" His voice had an edge to it I didn't recognize. For a second, I was worried it was the return of the power of Wrath inside him - but he didn't sound angry.

"That he could be there when you punish whoever killed Madaleine. I know it might not be possible, but I felt bad for him."

Nox stared at me, and his eyes were alarmingly bright. He had a wild, almost feral look to him, and I glanced at Behemoth, who was sitting on the leather car seat, also staring at Nox.

"Are you okay?"

"I saw his soul."

"Cornu's?"

"Yes. He is a demon. He should not have a soul."

"Okay... What does that mean? He's not actually a demon?"

"No. He is a demon." Nox snapped his intense eyes from mine to Behemoth. "I need you to leave us."

Behemoth blinked, then slowly shook his horned head. "I'm sorry, Lucifer. I am not permitted."

Nox stared a moment, then spoke. "Fine. Claude! Stop the car."

The moment the vehicle stopped moving, Nox flung open the door, grabbed my arm, and pulled me out of the car. I didn't even have time to see where we were before his wings unfurled and he bent, scooping me up.

I gasped as he crouched, then launched us into the air.

"Nox! Where are we going?" I had to shout over the rushing wind, pressing my face into his shoulder as he banked hard, left then right.

"Where we can be alone. Truly alone." We were moving so fast I couldn't see, for the whipping of my hair around my face and the freezing air making my eyes stream.

Just moments later we slowed, and I peeked over his shoulder, breathing hard.

Big Ben.

With a tiny thud, he landed on top of the gargantuan clock. "Nox! We can't be up here!" He tipped me from his arms, so I was standing, but pulled me close immediately, gripping the tops of my arms.

"Look at me."

I did, still breathless. He looked even wilder than he had in the car. "What's wrong?"

"He loved her."

"What?"

"He loved her. He doesn't want to live without her."

"Cornu?"

"Yes. He shouldn't be able to love like that. You need a soul to love like that."

"You just said he had a soul."

"He does, now. But he was not created with one."

I frowned in confusion. "You're saying Madaleine made him a soul somehow?"

"No. *Love* made him a soul."

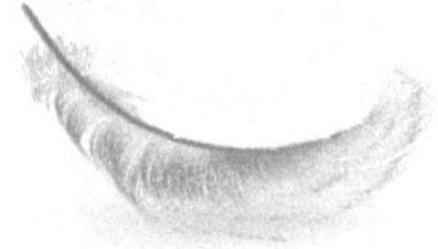

TWENTY-ONE

NOX

What I had seen inside Cornu... He had lost love. The woman he would give his life for had been taken, for good. And it had shattered him. The fragile, forbidden soul that love had given him, splintered beyond repair.

My fear of losing Beth ran so hot and fast through me that my ears rang, and my mind was clouded. She was all I could see in the fog. "I want you next to me for eternity. I'd turn the whole fucking world to ash, if you asked me to. I cannot do anything if you are not happy. I will save you. From everything. And I think you might be able to save me."

She stared into my face, her beautiful eyes filled with that honest emotion I couldn't get enough of. "I think I've fallen in love with you." Her voice shook as she spoke, and her hand pressed tight to my jaw. The rest of the world melted away, and the ringing in my ears got louder.

"Love." I repeated the word as the fog in my mind

thickened, her face before me so crystal clear in comparison. "Love." With blinding clarity, I understood it. It transcended every emotion I had ever felt, eclipsing Lust, Greed, Wrath—the strongest powers I'd ever had. It encompassed my entire being, and it was fucking glorious. "I didn't think the devil was capable of love," I breathed, moving my hands to her face, pulling her even closer. "I was wrong."

She closed the gap between us, pressing her lips to mine. My Lust power had always been able to elevate a kiss by letting me bare my soul and my desires. But this kiss was on another level entirely.

Fire burst to life in my chest as the fog cleared completely, and I lost myself completely to the strength of her passion. *Her love.*

Something inside me had changed.

I needed her. I needed her like I needed water, or food. Except, unlike food, I could actually taste her. And her flavor was exquisite. Made for me. Destined. Fated. Mine, and mine alone to feast on.

Every priority I had lived my life by had disintegrated. Every tug of emotion that wasn't connected to her was meaningless. She had to be safe. She had to be happy. And if she could be by my side, then the gaping fucking hole inside my soul would finally heal. I would be complete.

She moved her head, hands still on my face, staring into my eyes. "I love you," she said, as though the words were a deliciously forbidden fruit.

"I love you," I breathed back. Words I never thought I *could* say.

I wrapped my arm tight around her, beat my wings, and launched us from the top of the enormous clock.

TWENTY-TWO

BETH

I gasped as Nox lifted us from the top of Big Ben. My mind was reeling, utter joy mingled with desire so intense I was unable to think straight.

Nox was mine. He loved me.

I thought maybe he had loved me as long as I'd loved him, but hadn't believed it possible. Whatever he had seen within Cornu had shattered that.

I melted in his grasp; my hands anchored around his neck as we rose higher over London. His mouth found mine as his wings beat, and I tasted sweet oblivion. My greedy body wanted it all.

I needed him. He was mine, and I was his, and there was nothing in my head except being one with him. Showing him how much I loved him, how real and true this was.

He kissed me even harder, and every nerve ending felt like it was on fire. I rocked into his grip needing stimulation, friction, anything to ease the ache in my core. Ease the absence of him. Ease the need beating me down with each masterful stroke of his tongue on mine.

I knew he wouldn't let me fall. He held me tight against him, and my legs wrapped around his waist, up under his wings.

He slowed, and his ferocious kisses moved, trailing down my jaw, then neck.

I was vaguely aware that dusk was falling around us. I adored London, and the view of it coming to life with lights as I soared high above it wrapped in the arms of the man I loved, caused unbridled joy to fill me. I felt like I was in a dream. A dream I hoped never to wake from.

Nox moved, shifting his grip on me, and I tore my gaze away from the beauty below to stare into his eyes. There was so much more beauty right here within my grasp.

He met my look with pure desire.

"Nox." I whispered his name like a prayer. Each sweep of his mouth on my skin set me on fire, burning through any doubts I had, any fears, any notion that I'd ever have to let him go.

"I love it when you say my name," he growled. "I want to hear it every time I make you come. Every time."

His words made me breathe his name again.

"I need to touch you," he said against my lips, his arms wrapped so tight around me an ache started in my ribs.

I reached up to sweep my flying hair out of my face. "Do it."

A smile curled at the corner of his mouth, and he shifted me in his grasp to bring one hand down the curve of my waist.

Expertly, he unfastened the fly on my jeans, then delved his hand inside. In seconds he was parting my aching flesh with his fingers, stroking my wetness. His eyes stayed locked with mine, the city twinkling to life in the dark beyond his glowing wings.

A dream. It's all an exquisite dream.

He's a dream.

My dream.

He's mine.

His fingers dipped inside me and then swirled up to circle my clit as if he'd done it a thousand times. He knew exactly how to touch me and how hard I wanted it.

"Does that feel good?"

I dropped my head against his shoulder, the wind cutting through my moans.

When I didn't answer, he spoke again.

"Look at me. I want to see you break apart in my arms. I want to feel it as I see it spark in your eyes."

I swallowed hard, needing to make room for more oxygen. He nodded once and pressed his lips to mine as his hand delved back into my panties. With one smooth stroke of his fingers after another, I felt myself panting, pleasure firing through me, building. He captured every sound I made with his mouth, his eyes burning a promise into my soul.

"That's right. Come apart in my arms."

His words were my undoing. My eyes rolled back in my head.

"I love to watch you come," he whispered in my ear.

I gasped his name, then cried out his name. He thrust his tongue into my mouth, sending me over the edge. I shattered for him, an endless loop of pleasure that went on and on.

"Good," he murmured, catching my lips on his. "So good."

I'd never come like this, not in my life.

"You're stunning," he growled.

I tilted my head back to look at him. Words failed me. Words, breath, thought. Everything.

"What are you thinking?" he asked me, his voice laced with need.

"That I love you."

Light fired in his eyes, then he clutched me tight to him, and dove.

I shrieked as air rushed past us, adrenaline blasting through me, adding to the sensations already wracking my body.

We were on the ground in seconds, and I gripped him as he carefully set me on my feet. I was vaguely aware that we were on his rooftop, on the small area of lawn.

In a rush, we were tearing at each other's clothes and just seconds later, we were skin to skin on the grass. I was trembling with anticipation as Nox stepped back, his muscular chest heaving.

Slowly, he took me in from the top of my head to the tips of my toes, and I felt a jolt of need slam into me as I saw my own desire so intensely reflected back at me in his eyes.

He moved his hand to his erection, and I stared, transfixed. "I'm going to take you hard. I want to feel every inch of your body shuddering around me. Will you come for me again, Beth? Scream my name while I take you?"

I nodded. "Yes. Yes," I said, my voice shaking.

"I want to hear it."

"I'll come for you. I'll scream your name."

"Mine," he growled. "Say it again."

"Yours," I said, my voice no more than a whisper. "I'm yours."

"Again," he said, his voice thick with desire.

"Yours." I said it loud, loud enough for the whole city to hear.

"Mine."

"Always."

He stepped forward and grabbed my hand, bringing it up to his mouth, kissing my palm and fingers and wrist and every inch in between.

"I'm yours, too, Beth."

I moaned as his kisses moved up my forearm, the cool night air accentuating the softness of his touch.

"I'm yours," he said against the skin of my breast as his lips moved.

His warm tongue flicked over my nipple, sending shocks of pleasure straight to my center, and making me moan louder.

He wrapped an arm around my waist, lifting me. I

lifted my legs around his hips and he lowered us to the ground so I straddled his lap. His hard cock pressed against my still swollen clit, and I gasped.

He trailed his hand up the ridge of my spine until he reached my hair, pulling my ass closer to him with his other.

"I will never stop pleasuring you, Beth. And the feel of your pussy around me will never be anything less than exquisite. You will always feel this. You will never need anyone else the way you need me. Your body will always crave mine, and whenever I touch you, you'll remember that, always. I'm going to make you mine in every way."

"Nox."

"Tell me what you want."

"I want you to fill me. Make me yours. Show me how much you love me."

He put one hand on my neck, tilting my chin to look at him. The moonlight spilled over his face, his eyes full of need. "I do love you. I will keep loving you—forever, Beth. Forever."

His voice was thick with emotion. I could feel the truth behind his words. I could feel how much he loved me, and I could feel his consuming need to consume me.

"Please, Nox. Please."

He let go of my neck and grabbed my waist, lifting me higher on his lap. I felt the head of his cock slide through my wetness and I shuddered.

"You're so wet for me."

He rubbed the head against my clit and I groaned, my hips rising and falling against him, desperate for more.

"That's it," Nox said, watching me as I ground myself against his hardness, my breasts pressing into his solid chest. "I want you to come again."

My body pulsed with pleasure. I wanted him inside me so bad, but the waves of pleasure were building so fast, I couldn't stop myself.

"Come for me."

His words sent me over the edge, and I cried out as my orgasm slammed through me.

"Mine," Nox breathed, then pushed into me.

I gasped as I felt him fill me, inch by inch, taking me slowly, letting his thickness grow inside me. My overly-sensitive body shuddered around him, my nails digging into his shoulders.

"Look at me."

I did, staring into his eyes, his beautiful bright eyes, filled with love for me.

He buried himself to the hilt, his body shaking with mine.

"You feel so good, Beth. So good."

He pulled my head to him, kissing me, his tongue invading my mouth, and I lost all control of my body. My hips started to move on their own, and I rode him, my body clenching and releasing around his cock.

"Fuck, Beth. You're so beautiful."

I kissed him back and rode him faster, my need for him overwhelming me.

I didn't even think the last orgasm I'd had was over, and I cried out, my entire body tensing as pleasure crashed into me again. I could feel my walls pulsing around him, and then he was thrusting, picking up speed, his hips rocking into mine. I clawed at his chest, digging my fingers into him, desperation coursing through me. I felt his muscles bunch beneath my fingers, felt his thrusts getting faster, more desperate.

I wanted him to lose control with me. I wanted to be with him forever.

"Beth…" he breathed, his voice so thick with pleasure. "Beth…"

I moaned, my nails digging into his flesh, wanting to hold on to him, but it wasn't enough. I wanted more. I wanted him. His body. His heart. His soul.

"You're mine, Beth. I'm never letting you go."

I felt his hand slip between our bodies and his thumb found my clit. He started circling the little nub. My body quickened, and I could feel my orgasm rising, along with his. I moved into every thrust he gave me, and when he pinched my clit, I lost it.

I cried out, and then I was coming and coming and coming. My body tensed and jerked and I spasmed around him.

"Fuck," he growled.

"Come for me," I whispered, my body twisting and shaking from the pleasure of his thrusts. His body hardened. He pulled me to him, holding me tight, then roared and jerked beneath me. I could feel him pulsing and throbbing inside me, then the warmth of his come filling me.

I collapsed into his shoulder, utterly spent, waves of

pleasure still hammering through me, and he wrapped both arms tight around me, breathing hard.

I was his, and he was mine.

TWENTY-THREE

BETH

I hadn't even realized that I'd drifted off until I awoke, pressed tight against Nox. I moved gently, not wanting to wake him, and his arm squeezed my waist, stopping me completely.

"Hey," I said, leaning back into him.

"Hi." I rolled under his arm so I was facing him and kissed his neck. "Beth, we need to talk."

He must have felt me freeze, because he sat up quickly, scooping me up and pulling me with him. He cupped my cheek, staring into my eyes. His shone in the gloom, and my stomach lurched. I loved him. No question, doubt or regret. I loved him.

"You are mine. Forever," he said. "And we need to talk about how we make that happen. I can't go back to Hell."

I sucked in air, relief thwacking me in the gut. "What can we do?"

"We have to lift the curse. I... I think the effects of us being together are getting stronger."

"Oh no, I've hurt you-" I started, but he brushed his thumb over my lips, stilling my words.

"More power has moved than before. Your wings are really something," he smiled. "Stunning, in fact."

I swallowed. Now that he said it, I did feel that burning ball of power in my chest, stronger than before. "What happens when we lift the curse?" I asked again, unsure what else to say.

"Four things. Hopefully five." He kept one hand stroking slowly up and down my neck, twining his fingers in my hair when he reached it. He held his other hand up and began ticking off the points on his fingers as he spoke. "Number one. We find out who has been trying to remove me from power. They will be forced to face me directly, or back off, once I am at full strength. Number two; we find your parents. Number three; I use my divine negotiating skills to work out a deal with Examinus. Number four; we find a way a way to make you immortal."

I drew in an even bigger breath. "That's a serious to-do list."

"It is. But we can do it."

"What about Banks?"

"That's number five."

I nodded. "Nox, do you really think Examinus will let you out of Hell?" When I had mentioned Examinus letting him go before Nox had been adamant it wouldn't happen. I didn't know what had caused his change of attitude. Love-fueled optimism perhaps?

"We have options."

"We do?"

"We do, if you are right about my brother caring for me."

"What do you mean?"

"If Gabriel is willing to help, then we might be able to get some leverage on Examinus. Something I can use to bargain with him."

This was definitely a change in attitude. "A couple days ago you thought Gabriel was the one trying to kill you."

"He still might be. But if he's not, and you've read him as well as you read Cornu and Madaleine, then it's the best chance we've got. And I'm inclined to trust your instincts, Miss Abbott."

That lovely blanket of warmth wrapped around me at his words. The respect of a man like Nox was the best freaking aphrodisiac in the world.

"And then, we'll find a way to make you live forever."

I dropped his gaze, snagging my lip between my teeth. I really, really wasn't sure how I felt about that. The idea was too alien to even process.

He picked up my hand, locking his fingers between mine and pressing it to his chest. To his heart. "I want you to have this for as long as it beats, Beth."

A golf-ball sized lump grew in my throat. "But-" I started, but he squeezed my hand tighter in his, against his solid body.

"I can't bear to lose you. And you don't want to know what destruction I might cause if I ended up in Cornu's state." He gave me a teasing smile, trying to lessen the gravity of what we were talking about. "You're obligated to live as long as me Beth, to save humanity from my grief."

I gave him a look, but really, I was grateful for him turning the conversation playful. Even if we both knew there was an element of truth to his words. The memory of Cornu's broken spirit made the lump return.

"Nox?"

"Beth."

"I love you." Saying the words was like a hit of a drug, lifting me into a place where I was invincible. A safe place, where all my focus shifted to him, and my thoughts couldn't spiral out of control. Somewhere where, together, we could be anything, do anything. Conquer worlds. Pleasure each other until there was nothing else left. Dance. *Anything we wanted.*

"I love you," Nox answered, and my eyes burned. Romance had always made me cry, but I was used to other people's stories. To have the love of this man, in real life... This love story belonged to me.

Everything had changed. Abruptly, that one day I walked into his office, then exquisitely slowly ever since. And now, my fate was utterly bound to his. I would go wherever he went, as I knew he would go with me. I would never tire of him, and somewhat astonishingly, I knew he never would of me. I wasn't boring Beth to him. I wasn't sure I was boring Beth to *me* anymore either.

His power inside me had awoken my lost hope. It had found the parts of my soul that had broken, piece by piece, year by year, as I looked for my parents and failed. It had balked at the way I had let myself be used, too spent to fight any more.

And it had drawn all those pieces back together, gathering kindling for a burning fire that had been dormant for too long.

My lost hope was back, strong and fierce and full. And it stretched beyond finding my parents.

I was worthy of Nox. I was the woman who completed him. The only woman. *His woman.*

And I was ready to fight for my man.

TWENTY-FOUR

BETH

I didn't wake the next day until bright light forced my reluctant eyelids open.

"Rise and shine, beautiful."

I felt weight beside me and blinked the sleep from my eyes. Nox sat on the edge of the bed, dressed in suit trousers and a shirt. The curtains were open, and light flooded the room.

"Hello. Are you going to work?" I mumbled thickly.

"I've just got back from work," he said, leaning down to kiss my cheek.

"What? What time is it?"

"Two pm."

"Shit!" I sat bolt upright, making myself a little dizzy, and Nox laughed.

"Are you worried your boss is going to sack you for being late?"

I reached out, punching him. The movement made the bedclothes fall from my chest. A hungry look filled his eyes as he looked down my body, then back to my face.

"I fear a repeat of last night would actually kill me, so you'd better put those beautiful breasts away, before I do something stupid," he growled.

I groped for the sheet. "Are you a lot weaker?" I asked, guilt wracking me.

"It was worth it."

I sat straighter, clutching the sheet to my chest. *No self doubt. No regrets.*

"I woke you because Behemoth wants to talk to you."

"Oh god." Nerves trickled through me. What if our declaration of love had cost us the lead on the book?

Memories of last night played in my mind and I clutched the sheet tighter.

He loves me. I love him. We were eternal.

If we lost the lead, it had been worth it. *One hundred percent worth it.*

"Where is he?"

"Downstairs. It turns out he'd never tried coffee before. I should warn you now, if you thought that goat was hyper before caffeine, you haven't seen anything like this."

Nox hadn't been exaggerating. Behemoth was nuts.

"I am glad you are here," he said as I entered the kitchen. He was trotting around in a circle on the tile floor, next to Beelzebub, who was laying down with his tongue hanging out and staring at the goat. Nox pushed a coffee across the counter toward me, then folded his arms, a grin on his face. I thanked him before turning back to Behemoth.

"I see you made friends with Beelzebub."

"Yes. He is not very bright, but he beats talking to the stone. And he can run almost as fast as I can." The miniature goat changed direction, trotting anti-clockwise.

"Right. Nox said you wanted to talk? Am I in trouble?"

"Techa wishes to see you."

I looked at Nox and saw him tense. "When?" he barked.

"Now. Here. If you will permit?"

Nox's face turned dark, but I spoke before he could. "Please, Nox. Let's get this over with."

He looked at me a second, then nodded.

My skin turned icy cold, and then, in a haze of purple, Techa appeared next to Behemoth. He stopped trotting.

"What a pleasant surprise," Nox said, making it clear that it was no such thing.

"I am not here to converse with you," she said, and turned to me instead. I braced myself for the reprimand. "I am informed that you showed true compassion to a grieving creature others would have dismissed. And Behemoth believes that you are truly trying to reinstall Lucifer in his proper place, for the right reasons." She threw Nox a sideways glare and handed me an envelope. "These are tickets to a charity auction at the British Museum, tonight. The auction is being run by The

Collector. He bought the book from me. The auction is your best chance at pinning him down. In a good mood."

"Thank you," I said, in a rush of breath so loaded with relief that the words didn't come out right.

"I should thank *you* for helping remove this blight from London." She waved her hand at Nox, and he gave her one of his most outrageous smiles. She rolled her eyes.

"Behemoth's stone, please," she said, and held her hand out.

I felt a sharp pang of resistance, my initial relief fading. "But..."

"You do not need to be observed anymore."

"Right. Of course. Yeah." I fumbled in my pocket for the black and gold egg stone. It heated in my hand as I held it, and I curled my fingers around it involuntarily.

Techa cocked her head at me, then looked at Behemoth. "Is she concerned about the loss of the amplification of her powers?" She asked him as though I wasn't even there.

Behemoth blinked. "No. I think she is concerned about the loss of me."

"Really?"

I nodded. "I kinda like him."

The beautiful genie regarded me. "Behemoth, do you wish to remain in this mortal's company longer?"

"A little longer would not be a bad thing," said the goat.

"Fine. He can stay with you until you retrieve the book."

"Thank you," I said, putting as much sincerity as I

could into the two words. This time, they came out clearly.

"Call me, if you need me, Behemoth," she said, then vanished.

I blinked, looking between Nox and the goat.

"I thought she would be mad that we left you yesterday."

"It gave me an opportunity to tell her how you treated Cornu. She was as impressed as I thought she would be," Behemoth said, resuming his circles.

I looked at the little Hell-goat and turned the stone over in my hand. It heated pleasantly again. "Are you sure you don't mind hanging around with us a while longer?"

"I mind," said Nox ruefully, but he was smiling.

"Truthfully?" said Behemoth, pausing and turning his huge eyes to me.

I nodded at him. "Nothing but the truth here," I said.

"The presence of the Lord of Hell is pleasurable for any Hell-creature, and I won't deny that makes your company desirable, but that is not why I want to stay. I can't help feeling like you need me."

"Need you?" I raised my eyebrows and stopped myself asking what he thought he could do for me that Nox couldn't.

"Yes. I have a strong suspicion that my magnificence may soon be required."

"Nothing to do with seeing my friend who pets you again, then."

"No. Nothing at all."

"Right."

"As I am no longer needed to observe you now, you may send me into the stone when you desire privacy. Although, I am happy to amuse myself while we are in your home. I like to converse with your pet."

I shook my head, a grin spreading across my face.

"May I see those tickets?" Nox held his hand out and I passed him the envelope. He scanned them quickly. "The Collector is a very significant man in London. This is a big event." He looked at me, eyes shining. "You're going to need a dress. I'll meet you at about seven, and Rory and Behemoth will stay with you until then."

"I'm sure they'll love Behemoth at Liberties of London."

Fortunately, the store assistants at Liberties *did* love Behemoth. He was quite the little charmer when he wanted to be.

Rory hadn't been what I would call happy, exactly, to be helping me buy a dress again. But she definitely didn't look as annoyed as usual.

She treated shopping like a military operation, and I guessed the staff knew what to expect because they responded instantly to her, nabbing items from rails as though they had been put there purely for her perusal.

She was buying herself a dress for the evening too, and after an hour in the store, I was sure that she was secretly enjoying herself.

. . .

When I put the dress on in my room at Nox's an hour later, I was glad I'd followed my gut - as well as Rory's advice - and bought something to reflect my new confidence. There was no way I would have worn a dress like this a month ago.

It was scarlet red, and the top half was a close-fitting T-shirt shape, made of very fine, sheer fabric. Across my chest, hiding my breasts, was a burst of scarlet and burgundy sequins, reaching up toward my throat and down toward my navel in a subtle ombre, flower shapes woven into the sequins. The skirt of the dress started at my hips and burst out with enough volume to make me feel like I was in period drama. Or a Disney film. The bottom of the floor-length skirt was weighted with a big ruffle, and the urge to spin around was killing me. Giving in to it, I twirled. The skirt puffed out, reaching its full volume and flying around me in a riot of red.

I couldn't keep my delighted laugh in as I pirouetted to a stop in front of the closet mirror. I twitched my shoulder blades, and stared, enthralled as my gold wings rustled. Gold and red were a *great* combo.

"I love this dress."

"Yes. I can see that," said Behemoth.

I spent nearly an hour doing my hair and make-up, Behemoth chatting amiably the entire time. I tried to stick with the Disney princess vibe and pinned my hair up high on my head after curling it. If I'd had a tiara at hand, I might just have pulled the princess look off, I thought as I checked my reflection.

The sheer fabric at my stomach and shoulders was enough to make the dress a little sexy, but mostly it looked... Fierce.

I felt amazing in it.

"So. How do I look?"

"I am a magnificent Hellbeast, and not particularly adept at human fashions. But it is my belief that men will want to have sex with you."

There was a knock on the bedroom door. My stomach fluttered with excitable nerves when I went to answer it, but it wasn't Nox. It was Rory.

"Well. I see I nailed it again," she said, casting an assessing eye up and down. "You look like Belle, if she wore blood red." If I was Belle, then Nox was the beast. I decided to ignore the comparison.

"Behemoth's assessment was that men will want to have sex with me," I told her.

"If they want Nox to rip their bollocks off, then they're welcome to have a go."

"Yes. Well. You look great," I said, changing the subject. She did, too. She was wearing a white sateen gown, silky and heavy. The shoulder straps draped down, almost to her elbows, in contrast to the rigid bustier of the dress, and there was a high split on the left side of the long skirt.

"Thanks. Are you ready?"

"As I'll ever be."

"Where's Nox?" I asked as we got closer to the front

door of the house. I had seen no sign of him and couldn't smell his distinctive scent.

"He's sorting something out."

"Sorting what out?"

Rory looked over her shoulder at me, and I was surprised to see a rare smile before she spoke. "A surprise. For you."

TWENTY-FIVE

BETH

There was a white limousine outside the house, and it felt weird not being in Claude's car. It didn't take long to get to the British Museum, and my nerves grew as we neared the beautifully illuminated building. The structure was massive, with a squat, triangular carving over the main entrance, making it look like an ancient Greek temple. It was a stunning building without the glowing amber lights that lit the columns holding up the roof - with them, it looked magical. Rolled out in front of the shallow steps was a red carpet, and lining that were hundreds of people with cameras.

"Shit, I didn't know this was such a big deal," I said, anxiety making my stomach churn.

"They're not all human," Rory said. "This evening is a magical event too. Upstairs for them, downstairs for us."

The car rolled to a stop, and I steeled myself as somebody opened the door from the outside. Slowly, carefully, I emerged from the car. Cameras flashed instantly, and I instinctively screwed my face up, avoiding the blinding flashes.

"Who the fuck is that?" I heard someone say.

"Dunno."

Somebody shouted a name, of a pop star I thought, and all the cameras swung away. I took a breath and Rory put a hand on her hip beside me.

"Mr. Nox!" The cameras swung back, and a familiar scent reached me before his warmth did. Nox stepped out of the darkness behind the car. And holy hell, did he look good.

Nox in a tuxedo should come with a health warning. Desire pulsed through me, and he smiled, and I knew he knew what I was thinking. And thanks to his power, I knew exactly what he thought of my dress. Lust radiated from him, and images of the previous night raced through my mind, making me press my thighs together.

When he reached us, he wrapped one arm gently around my waist and kissed me on the cheek. "You look divine," he breathed into my ear.

"You look pretty damn good yourself." He looked like James Bond, if James Bond had a darker edge, and was significantly filthier.

He proffered me his elbow, and we walked up the red carpet, people yelling questions at him as we went. Most of them were about who I was. He ignored them all.

When we got to the end of the carpet, Nox stopped, and turned to the cameras, pulling me close to his side.

"Smile," he said to me. "I want everyone to see how beautiful you are and know that you're mine." His mouth barely moved as he said the words, ensuring that they were just for me. I beamed at him, and his eyes filled with light. "Perfect."

We posed for the cameras, and with Nox's arm around me and the gorgeous dress on, I felt less out of place than I ever would have imagined.

Just behind us, Rory had on her best bored face, and Behemoth was prancing around like a peacock. I didn't know how many of the paparazzi could see him, or Rory for that matter, but he didn't seem to care. He was a natural.

When a movie star got out of a car at the other end of the red carpet, we took our chance to get inside. I gaped at the space as we entered. Unlike the outside, it was completely modern. We were in a room shaped like a ring, the center of which was a white plaster structure with tall black windows. Everything was painted white except the ceiling, which was glass and covered in a latticework of lead strips. It bulged out above us, amplifying the feeling of being inside a circular tube.

"It's awesome," I said, staring up at it.

"You've never been here before?" Nox asked.

"Being an analyst at LMS was hard work," I grinned at him. "Never had time."

"Wait till you see the Egyptian mummies."

"Are they real? Like actual dead people in them?"

"Yes. Really old ones."

I pulled a face.

"Good evening, Mr. Nox. A pleasure to see you here. Do you have your invitation, please?" A young woman dressed in a tuxedo held her hand out to Nox expectantly. He fished the invitations out of his pocket and handed them to her. "Lovely. The Collector is delighted you could make it. Your party is downstairs tonight. You'll be given a paddle for the auction on your way through."

We thanked her and followed her pointed arm to a set of doors leading off the left of the building. We were handed glasses of champagne as we stepped through by more smartly dressed staff members.

"That's the Rosetta stone," Nox said as we approached a massive piece of rock behind glass. When we got close I saw that the whole thing was covered in inscriptions. "All language can be traced back or translated using what they've found on that stone over centuries."

"Wow. Is it magic?"

Nox shook his head. "No. Just smart human history. But the man who runs the magical part of this museum is known as the Collector, and he has more magical artifacts than most. I'm sure a few will be on sale tonight."

"You in the market for anything?"

His eyes flashed. "A book, as it happens," he half-growled, and I remembered the actual reason we were here. Easy to forget, with the dramatic entrance.

TWENTY-SIX

BETH

We followed the slow-moving trickle of people to the back of the room, where a cocktail bar had been set up between two enormous statues of Greek gods. Little round tables and high stools had been strategically placed between smaller statues and displays. "I have a surprise for you," said Nox.

"What is it?"

He pointed. There at the bar, dressed beautifully in a gold ruffled dress, was Francis.

I looked delightedly at Nox, then back at Francis. Holding her elbow gently in one hand, and toasting a glass to hers in his other, was Claude.

"Are they on a date?"

Nox grinned as he nodded and the boyish look on his face made my insides melt.

"This is my surprise?"

"Do you like it?"

I pressed my lips to his in answer. "It's the most perfect thing ever."

"Beth!" Everyone looked as Francis squealed my name as she noticed me.

"Are you having a nice time?" I asked her when we reached her.

"Are you shitting me? How, exactly, is it possible to have a bad time here? The booze is free!"

I laughed. "You look amazing."

"I know! I haven't worn this dress in years. To tell you the truth, it doesn't quite do up in the back, but Claude has promised that he is handy with safety pins, if I decide to allow him to take it off later."

Claude flushed a deep red, flicked his eyes to Nox, and downed his drink.

We found a table we could all stand around, and I took in the impressive hall. There were people I recognized everywhere, from movies, TV, and the covers of their albums or their social media videos.

I didn't spend a massive amount of time on social media myself. Recipe and book groups were about the extent of my online interactions. But the viral videos didn't escape me entirely, and I recognized a woman who I knew had a make-up channel that was massive, and a guy who played video games online for millions of viewers.

A woman wearing a stunning black gown that moved like liquid lace came over to us, batting her eyelashes at Nox and barely giving me or Rory a second glance. I guessed she wasn't magic, because her eyes didn't move to my wings, like a lot of guests' were.

"It's nice to see you, Mr. Nox," she gushed. "Are you here to buy anything in particular?" she gushed.

"No. I haven't looked at the catalogue," Nox replied.

She gave a gasp, then a giggle. "You're not supposed to admit that!" she mock whispered. "You naughty boy." Her smile turned predatory, and the heat in my chest roared to life. I could sense the Lust seeping from her as she took in Nox. Greed was there too, I realized. She wanted more than his body. She wanted his wealth, and his stature too. I stepped forward, looping my arm through Nox's.

"Hi," I smiled. "I'm Beth."

"Oh. I'm Suzy Fairport. I own Digital Media Diaries. What do you do, Beth?"

The challenge was clear. She had a good job. I was supposed to better it, or step down. "Research."

"What kind?"

I scrabbled for an answer that wasn't 'attempting to track down lost magical shit for the devil'. "Financial."

Understanding flashed on her face. "At LMS Financial Services?"

I nodded.

"So Mr. Nox here is your boss." She smiled smugly as she realized I was just an employee of the insanely hot and wealthy bachelor before her.

"And her lover," Nox said.

I felt my cheeks stretch into a smile, as the woman's expression turned pinched.

"Oh. Right. Good for you!" she said awkwardly. "Well, I must go. Goodbye."

She swept away.

"I want to get rid of the next one," I said quietly to Nox, still grinning.

He flashed me a wicked smile of his own. "You got it."

Together, we fended off a barrage of flirtatious women for the next half hour. I slowed down on the champagne, worried I might get too cocky in my public claiming of Nox. I was starting to enjoy it though. Gorgeous woman after gorgeous woman made her excuses and left after it being made perfectly clear that Nox was with me. And hell, it was making me feel good.

I looked over at the little table where Claude and Francis were now sitting. Francis had her head tipped back, belly-laughing at something, and Claude's eyes were sparkling as he watched her.

"You know, there might actually be a thing there."

"Shall I help them along?" Nox said, his own eyes flashing. I hit him playfully on the arm.

"Don't you dare get involved."

He raised his eyebrows. "Too late for that. I set them up tonight."

I beamed at him. "I know." I looked back over at them. "But seriously, the last thing Francis needs is any extra lust. She's bad enough already."

"I'll get us some more drinks," Nox said, but as I

started to thank him, his relaxed demeanor vanished, his expression hardening.

"What's wrong?"

"Envy is here. I can sense the power."

"Oh my god, really?" I couldn't keep the excitement from my own voice. "Nox, that's great!"

Rory leaned in. "Did I just hear you say Envy was here?"

Nox nodded. "Something's off, though, the sin power doesn't feel right."

I frowned. "Do you know what she looks like?"

"No. I last saw her six decades ago. Her appearance will have changed in that time, no doubt."

"All we know is her social media handle," said Rory.

"What does her power do?"

"It makes people envious," she answered, speaking like I was ten years old and stupid. I threw her a scowl.

"No shit. You know what I meant. Can she do any other magic we should know about, or will she just make the people around her jealous?"

Nox answered me. "The power of Envy makes people behave irrationally. It makes them believe that those with success have not really earned it, and that they are not entitled to it. As much as it invokes a feeling of jealousy, it also invokes anger, indignation and self-right-eousness."

"Sounds charming," I said.

"I never enjoyed it."

It was easy to forget that Nox was the source of the power of the sins. Once again, the painting flashed into my mind. He represented the guardian of the dark, warring against the light. That evil, whether he wanted it or not, was supposed to be contained within him.

I chugged some of my champagne.

Nox tensed, heat wafting from him, and I looked around sharply as his power inside me burst to life. I could sense something. Someone.

Envy.

Everyone around us was starting to ooze jealousy. I couldn't hear their thoughts or anything, just felt a bone-deep sense of wanting what everyone else had, rolling from them all.

"Good evening, Lucifer. I am surprised you found your way here tonight."

The voice belonged to an exceptionally smart older gentleman, with a neat, dark beard, cold ice-blue eyes and a top hat on. Somehow, his tux was straighter and neater than everyone else's I'd seen. Beside him was a woman with wavy blonde hair and a long, emerald-green dress. She had a face like a doll, pert and perfect and beautiful. And she was the source of the power I could feel.

"Good evening," said Nox, his eyes flicking between the two of them. "I received an unexpected invitation. I believe you have something of mine."

So, this was the Collector. My nerves ratcheted up a notch as I realized how important this conversation was.

"I do, as a matter of fact."

My breath hitched. *Had we actually found it?*

"I wish it returned." Nox sounded completely cool, all business. Which was surprising, given that the man he was talking to was at the end of a chain of thefts of his property.

"That can be arranged. For a price." The Collector smiled at him, and it was a cold, cruel smile. "Meet me after the auction. By the Sphinx. We shall discuss it in private."

"Fine," Nox said, then nodded at the blonde woman. "Long time, no see," he said.

She gave him a smile as cold as the Collectors. "Lucifer."

"I've been looking for you."

"And I've been avoiding you. Your resident vampire geek has been a pain in my ass." There was a tension in her voice and her face that made me agree with Nox. Something wasn't right. The more I studied her though, the more I wanted nothing more in the world than to look like her. To live like her. *To be her.*

I shook myself, taking a sip of my drink and forcing down the feeling, focusing instead on Nox.

"So, are you here to purchase?" Nox's question was casual, and the Collector laughed.

"The games we play," he smiled. "Envy here is good at games. She used to be the best, in fact. But I'm afraid I outplayed her."

I could see the hatred in her eyes as she looked at him.

An energy began to tingle around us, in a way that felt tangible and not all unpleasant.

"I work for the Collector now," Envy said. There was poison in her words.

"Until the debt is worked off," he nodded. "I've found, as a buyer and seller of items, that a little boost of envy works wonders on my ability to fetch a good price and close a sale."

"You're using her to make people pay more money for stuff?" I couldn't help my exclamation, and everyone looked at me.

"I heard Lucifer had a new pet," the Collector mused, looking me up and down, gaze lingering on my wings. "A mortal, of all things. A mortal with golden wings."

"Are you being held against your will?" Nox asked Envy, ignoring the Collector's words, but showing a hint of anger in his voice for the first time.

Envy stared at Nox a beat, then shook her head. "It is a business arrangement."

"She signed on the dotted line, Lucifer. You, of all people, know how deals work." Nox looked at him, and again I was surprised how calm he was. I didn't feel calm. I felt outraged.

This asshole was parading Envy around at an auction to make everyone want to outbid the others, and she clearly didn't want to be here.

"Speaking of deals, perhaps when we negotiate the return of my book, we can discuss Envy's indenture too."

Envy's pretty face was furious. "I heard a rumor you were looking for the angels you gave your sins to, but I didn't think it was true. What do you want with me?"

Nox just stared at her, and her face paled.

"No. You can't seriously expect me to just give it up.

It's my life, Lucifer. I am what you made me, you can't just show up one day and take it all away." Fear laced the anger in her words, and for a moment, I felt sorry for her.

"That was always the deal, Envy. You knew that when you signed the paperwork."

The Collector stroked a hand down his thin beard. "How fascinating. This could get expensive for you, Lucifer."

"Then it's a good job I'm obscenely wealthy."

The Collector laughed. "Indeed. I will see you after the auction. Enjoy."

TWENTY-SEVEN

BETH

"Is it wrong that I feel bad for her?" I asked as they strode away, Envy casting a blistering look over her shoulder at us.

"I feel bad for her, stuck with that prick."

"But not that you want to take her power away?"

"It's not her power."

Rory stepped in close to us. "So, we couldn't find her all this time because the Collector was keeping her?"

"It seems so."

"Why would he let you see her tonight then?"

"He wants to sell her on?"

"You can't sell people," I snapped, and they both looked at me.

"Beth, angels, Saints or Fallen, are mostly immortal and have indefinite lifespans. They often bargain with indenture, as time is their one unlimited resource."

I tried to make sense of that in my head. "You offer time if you've got no money?"

"Essentially, yes. Envy got herself into trouble and offered up the use of her and her power for an amount of time to clear the debt. And Rory makes a good point. I'm the only one who would see Envy and recognize her power and know who she truly is. If he's been keeping her hidden all this time, why expose her tonight, when I'm here?"

"A trap," said Rory, voice grave.

"We were sent here by Techa—could she have set us up?"

Behemoth snorted. "Never. And she wouldn't have sent me with you if she had."

"Good point."

"Envy said herself that she had heard rumors I was looking for her. The Collector is an exceptionally greedy man. He may have just seen an opportunity to make more money from me."

I hoped to hell that was the case. If we could get the book and the Envy page from the Collector tonight, that would be a massive step forward. Pride would be all that was left.

The wait staff were moving through the crowd, pointing people through one of two sets of doors - I assumed one magical and one non-magical. We were sent through the doors on the left, down some wide stairs and into a large chamber laid with many round tables and a small, raised platform at one end. High windows were draped with heavy, red velveteen curtains laced with gold, and an elaborate chandelier hung overhead. Paintings hung on the wall, many of them abstract and bright, with a couple of serene portraits breaking up the color.

A young woman gave us numbered paddles, and we were shown to a table with our names on place markers.

"Why don't I have one?" grumbled Behemoth.

"I don't think miniature goats get their own seats here. Sorry."

"Rude," he huffed, and pushed his way under the tablecloth.

"Are you sulking under there?" I asked him as I sat down in my designated seat.

"No."

"Good. Because magnificent Hellbeasts don't sulk."

"I suppose not," he said, re-emerging from under the table.

"Can you do me a favor? Can you go for a little scout around the room and see if there's anything out of the ordinary?"

His eyes flashed as he padded his feet. "I shall do so immediately," he said, and trotted off purposefully.

Nox looked at me. "Did you do that just to make him feel better about not having a seat?"

"Yes. He's cute. I like him."

Nox leaned over and kissed my cheek softly. "You bemuse me."

"They spelled my name wrong," I said, picking up my place marker. "It says Beth Appott, instead of Abbott."

As I moved the card in my hand, I realized there was writing on the back of it. My breath caught. It was the same handwriting as before.

The writing that looked just like my mom's.

Buy the ruby necklace. Whatever you do, you must buy the ruby necklace.

"Nox," I hissed. I showed him the card. "What do we do? Do you think it's from my mom?"

"I don't know. Bid on the necklace. Buy it," he answered, voice low and husky.

I nodded.

"Beth!" Behemoth's voice sounded in my head and I looked around for him. The room was filling up, most tables hosting their guests now, and I couldn't see him.

I answered him out loud, feeling a bit stupid, and having no idea if he could hear me. "Behemoth?"

"Cornu is here."

"What?"

"I don't know how he got in, but he's sitting at a table with a place name of something very different to his own."

"Is he drunk?"

"No. In fact, he looks pretty good."

Nox raised his eyebrows at me. "Fucking demons. If he messes up anything tonight, I'll send him back to Hell for good."

. . .

Before I could reply, the lights dimmed and the platform was illuminated with small spotlights. The Collector stepped out on the stage, stopping behind a wooden lectern. He was clearly our auctioneer for the evening.

"Welcome, my fine magical guests," he said in his clipped accent. "We are gathered here tonight for the auction of the century."

It took a while to get going, but once it did, bidding was hot. Envy stood beside the Collector, brandishing each item for sale. If there wasn't much of a reaction from the audience then the Collector would usher her further into the room so that she could walk between the tables, showing off the lots.

I watched as the first few were sold: an enormous grandfather clock that was painted with blue eagles for five thousand pounds, a dress that changed color for two thousand pounds, and a broadsword, almost as tall as I was, for ten thousand pounds.

"And up next we have this stunning necklace. What do we think?"

The lights dimmed, and then brightened to reveal the necklace. "A ruby pendant, made up of two square panels of rubies set in white gold."

The room filled with gasps and excited chatter. It was gorgeous. I was so busy staring at it, I didn't even hear the first bid. Nox reached his hand under the table, and I started when he squeezed my thigh.

"If that's the necklace you're supposed to buy, you'd better start bidding," he whispered.

"Right," I said, my throat tight with tension.

My hand shot up in the air, and the Collector pointed in my direction.

"Ten thousand," he said.

"What?" I'd not realized how high the bidding had got already, and I felt sick as I looked at Nox. He grinned at me.

"Fifteen thousand," said a voice from the front.

"Thirty thousand," shouted a voice from across the room.

My throat was dry, and I could barely hear anything over the sound of my own pulse.

"Nox, I can't afford this!"

"I can. Which means you can."

The heat in my chest flared, desire for the beautiful jewelry just as strong as the desire to beat everyone else to it.

I knew it was the power of Greed inside me, and no doubt, Envy's influence was adding to it.

But stronger than the sin powers was the knowledge that my Mom had told me to get the necklace. I was so sure the notes were from her.

"The lady bids fifty thousand dollars." I glanced up at the stage. A woman wearing a beautiful designer gown at the table at the front was holding up her paddle, nodding at the Collector. Nox squeezed my thigh again, and I raised my paddle.

"Do I hear fifty-five? Fifty-five?" He pointed to me. "Fifty-five here. Any more?"

"Fifty-six," said a gruff voice from the front.

"Sixty," I said, my voice shaking, my hand still in the air.

"Sixty-five," said the woman at the front.

"Sixty-six," I said, my palm sweating on the paddle.

"Seventy," said the gruff voice.

"Seventy-one," I said.

"Eighty."

"Eighty-one," I said.

"Ninety," he said, and I could hear the smile in his voice. My heart sank. He was going to get the necklace. I lowered my paddle and stared at it, knowing I'd lost.

"Why have you stopped?" Nox hissed.

"That's a huge amount of money," I whispered, and Nox took my hand and kissed it.

"Keep bidding."

I shook my head, swallowing back the voice screaming at me to take what I wanted. The voice fueled by Greed. "I can't. There's no way you can afford that."

"Yes, I can. And you have to buy it. Keep bidding."

I watched as the woman at the front went to ninety-five thousand.

"One hundred thousand," said Nox beside me.

"No!" I said, but at the same time Nox closed his hand around mine and raised our paddle. The Collector turned to us.

I stared at Nox, my mouth open.

"One hundred thousand for this stunning piece." The Collector pointed his hand at me. "From the young lady with Mr. Nox. Any more?" he said, looking around the room.

Envy walked slowly past the woman at the front table, dangling the sparkling piece of jewelry before her. But the woman's mouth formed a thin line and she shook her head. Envy changed direction, approaching the owner of the gruff voice. There was silence.

"Going once..."

I held my breath.

"Going twice... Sold. The ruby necklace is sold to the lady at table forty-four."

The lights dimmed, and the auction continued. I grabbed Nox's arm.

"Whoooooeee!" exclaimed Francis from the other side of the table. "Beth, you got a corker there! And I mean the necklace *and* the fella who can afford it for you!"

"Why did you spend so much money?" I hissed at Nox, trying to ignore her. "What if it's worthless, or a trick, or-" Nox cut me off by holding his finger up to my lips.

"I will have lost more than that by the end of the night and will make ten times that tomorrow."

I stared at him. Greed rumbled through me again,

images of living with that much money all the time tumbling gleefully through my mind.

Behave! I told the errant power. *We bought the necklace because we need it. Mom believes we need it. Not because it's so freaking beautiful...*

"And if it turns out to be nothing, you'll look fucking fantastic wearing it, and nothing else," Nox breathed, his hand skimming my inner thigh.

I sucked in a breath, the image seeping from his mind to mine. Me, sauntering toward him naked, the ruby glowing at my throat.

He was right. I did look fucking fantastic.

"Is that what I look like to you?" I whispered.

"No. That's what you look like in real life. You're stunning."

My face flushed with pleasure at his words. "Thank you."

"When we've got the Book and Envy's page back, then perhaps I can spend a bit more time convincing you."

TWENTY-EIGHT

BETH

"I wish they weren't here," Nox said.

We were standing by the sphinx, as instructed. But we weren't alone. Rory and Behemoth were kind of a given, but Francis and Claude were additions we hadn't been able to get rid of. The best we'd managed was to make them stand ten feet away, in front of a smaller statue of a scarab beetle. They were still chatting animatedly.

Francis saw me looking over and waved cheerily at me. "Just you let me know if you need our help, honey!" she hollered, unnecessarily loudly.

"Will do," I waved back. I turned back to Nox. "I'm sure she won't get in the way," I said, unable to keep the doubt from my voice. "She doesn't get out much."

"It's not her getting in the way I'm worried about. I like her. I wouldn't want anything to happen that would upset her. Or you."

My heart swelled. I loved that he liked Francis.

"She's pretty robust. If her stories are true, she's almost seen as much debauchery in her life as you have."

He gave me a dry smile.

"He should be here by now. He's keeping me waiting on purpose."

Once the auction had ended, everyone else had been invited to an after party at a nearby bar. We were the only people I had noticed move deeper into the museum, instead of leaving it. Well, that wasn't entirely true.

"Is Cornu still hiding behind that pillar?" I asked Nox.

"Yep."

The demon must have known that Nox could sense him, but he hadn't opted to make himself known to us. Nox had suggested we just let him follow us, rather than risk drawing the Collector's attention to our stalker. Likely Cornu just wanted to make sure he didn't miss an opportunity to see his revenge exacted.

"Lucifer." The Collector appeared in the archway at the other end of the room. Envy was next to him, and she had glowing cuffs on. "I apologize for my tardiness; I had an escape attempt to deal with." Envy glowered at him, and I felt a stab of guilt. I'd probably have tried to run too, if I was about to be sold on and have my magic powers taken away.

The Collector and Envy stopped when they reached us, and he cast a brief eye over Francis and Claude. They had fallen quiet and were staring at our group.

"I must say, you are keeping some odd company these

days," he said with a small shake of his head. "Is that a miniature Hell-goat?"

"Yes. He's not for sale."

"Shame. I believe this is yours, madame," he said, and nodded his head at Envy. Reluctantly, she held up a large black box with the ruby necklace in it.

"Oh. Thank you." I reached for it. The box was too big for my purse, and Envy shook her head.

"Just put it on."

I opened my mouth to argue, but as I looked at the necklace, I decided she was probably right. It was beautiful, after all. I lifted it from the box and secured it around my neck.

"To business," the Collector said, moving his attention from me to Nox. "You want to buy the Book of Sins?"

"*My* Book of Sins. That was stolen and sold on illegally. Yes."

The Collector laughed. "I would run out of fingers to count on if I totted up the number of illegally procured items you yourself have put through my halls over the centuries, Lucifer."

"Name your price," Nox said. I could hear some tension starting to creep into his voice.

"Two million. And a sample of Mount Ignis."

I bit down on my tongue to keep my jaw from falling open. *Two million.*

"One million," Nox countered. "And I want Envy. You can have a sample from Mount Calidum instead."

"Two million and you can have Envy. I already have

samples from Mount Calidum, everyone does. They are worthless to me. It's Mount Ignis or nothing."

"It is not easy to get rock from Mount Ignis."

"I am well aware of that. That is why I want it."

There was a long silence and I was sure everyone would be able to hear my heart beating. "Fine," said Nox, eventually. "But no more than one and a half million."

"One seven five."

"I want the book first."

"Sign here." He produced a scroll from his sleeve and unfurled it with a flourish. Black ink flowed across the page, solidifying in a scrawl that I could just about decipher as the terms they had just agreed.

Nox pulled a pen from an inside pocket of his jacket and waved his hand. The scroll flew from the Collector's hand, hovering in front of him.

The second it was signed, the Collector beamed. "Off you go now," he said to Envy. "I will fetch the book. Wait here."

He marched back down the hall, and Envy glared at Nox.

"The page, please," he said to her.

"As if I'd have it with me," she spat.

"I know you have it with you. Give it to me now."

"I don't have it," she repeated, loudly.

"I will free you from the indenture and ensure that you are financially secure for the next three years if you give me the damn page now." She stared at him, eyes narrowing. "You have thirty seconds, Envy. I don't need to offer you anything at all in return, I could just compel you. But I would rather not."

"Trying to save my dignity, are you?" she said sarcastically. But the fight had left her, I could tell by the slump of her shoulders. She bent, hands still cuffed together. "You know, maybe getting rid of this fucking power won't be so bad. Maybe I'll get some peace for once."

"Maybe you don't need it anymore," I said. "Don't you have a pretty awesome following online now? I'm sure your fans will stay with you. They probably won't even notice anything is different."

She straightened her head to look up at me, and I saw that she was unfastening the strap of her sandal.

"Thanks for your words of wisdom, miss fucking optimistic," she muttered, then yanked her shoe from her foot. She pulled at the stiletto heel and to my surprise, it separated from the rest of the shoe with a snap, swinging on a hinge. She tipped it upside down, and a tiny rolled-up piece of paper slid out. She hesitated a second, and handed it to Nox.

His wings snapped out behind him instantly, and I heard Francis gasp.

Nox began to read from the page in Latin, fast, the shadows gathering quickly around him. He was wasting no time, and I guessed he didn't want the Collector present when he took his power back.

Shadows burst to life around Envy, pouring from her body, and fear filled her beautiful eyes before they closed, and her head tipped back.

Nox clapped his hands together, and the bright blue

light appeared between them as he drew them apart. The shadows rushed toward it, merging and swirling, before spreading to his wings. As before, the mass of dark power seemed to melt into his feathers, and within a moment, it was over.

Envy opened her eyes, and Nox's wings slowly retracted as he put the small piece of paper into his inside pocket.

"Thank you. I will have your funds transferred tomorrow."

Envy glared at him, then held up her cuffed wrists. Nox said something in Latin and touched them, and they vanished. She crouched, refastening her sandal, then whirled as she stood, avoiding looking at us. The click of her heels faded as she strode out of the hall.

Nox's eyes were shining when I looked at him. "One more to go," I breathed, trying to keep my voice calm. He was radiating power and was somehow even more alluring than he had been all evening.

Before he could answer, there was the sound of footsteps, this time, not stiletto heels.

"The Book of Sins," came the Collector's voice, and he emerged from behind the sphinx statue.

I narrowed my eyes as he got closer.

Greed was pouring from him, so thick and powerful it made it hard for me to concentrate on much else. *Why was he feeling so much Greed?* He hadn't felt this when Nox had signed the parchment.

I felt heat from Nox beside me and glanced sideways at him. He was as still as the statues surrounding us. *He felt it too.*

"As promised," said the Collector, stopping before the fifteen-foot sphinx and holding up a brown leather-bound book. Very slowly, he crouched down, and laid the book down on the tiled floor. "I hereby pass this book from my ownership to yours."

"Why is he putting it on the floor instead of giving it to you?" I hissed under my breath.

"Because this is a trap," Nox growled. Louder, so that the Collector could hear him, he continued. "He's putting it on the floor because he wants me to go and pick it up. His end of the deal is fulfilled. He has passed the book to me. Unfortunate that it is not in my hands yet. I should have read the fine print."

The Collector's eyes were gleaming when he looked up at us. Shadows flew from Nox, swirling into tight tornados and diving for the book. But yellow light sparked around it before they could reach.

"I'm going to need to take that." Another figure stepped out from behind the sphinx statue.

Banks.

The smell of sulfur crashed over me, and the hall was abruptly ten times hotter. I spun, reaching for Nox as every single instinct in my body screamed danger.

A Hellhound stalked along beside the sphinx, behind Banks.

Nox's wings burst from his back and Rory moved fast to Francis and Claude, her hands glowing pink.

The Collector's voice rang out through the hall. "Can I go now?" He was eyeing the Hellhound and moving slowly in the opposite direction of the beast.

"No," Banks said.

"You said I just had to get Lucifer here," he protested.

The Hellhound growled, and the Collector fell silent.

Nox's voice was granite. "Beth, I am not leaving here without the book. But you must. Now."

"Too late, Lucifer," Banks sang. His eyes cut to mine, and Nox growled deep in his chest. He moved like lightning, stepping in front of me so that he was between Banks and me, shadows pouring across his golden feathers as his wings stretched wide like a shield.

"Time to finish this, Banks." Power was rolling from him, the promise of a slow and painful death in every word he uttered. The shadows carried the sounds of screams, images of fire, making my knees tremble. The power inside me flared up, and the sensation lessened.

Banks laughed as the book floated in the air, still wrapped in his power. "Oh, little Lucifer. You truly have so little clue what you are dealing with. You are right - we will finish this. But you will lose."

Nox moved forward, advancing on him. The Hellhound ducked into a crouch beside Banks.

"Will you not fight me yourself?" Nox shouted. "Or are you two cowardly? I know you are controlling them with that symbol. Who gave you the Hell power to do that, Banks?"

"I don't need to fight you myself. I get to tear you apart once you are my captive, sin power by sin power."

Nox roared a laugh dripping with condescension. "You can't take my sin power, you weak little fool. You are a mere Fallen angel, and I am your damned Lord!"

Banks' eyes widened with as a mad grin spread across his face. "Oh, but I can. Examinus will be so pleased you found Envy," he hissed. Nox froze.

Examinus?

"Gloria was supposed to find it for him, but this makes things much easier."

Gloria?

Gloria was my mom.

TWENTY-NINE

BETH

"I suppose I should give her some credit, we wouldn't have been able to bribe the Collector here if she hadn't been involved."

I felt sick, my legs unsteady beneath me as my heart raced.

"Why?" My word was a croak.

"Examinus needs the book, the sins, and Lucifer here. The full set. He knew you would be too stupid to discover that Max had been to the Natural History Museum, and he could hardly enter the human realm and question the genie himself, could he? So, he sent Gloria to give you Max's ticket, the one person your little pet mortal couldn't resist trusting."

"You're lying."

He had to be lying.

"Oh, Gloria!" His call was in a singsong voice, and my breath stuttered in horrified anticipation. With a small fizz of green light, my mom appeared beside him.

"No. No, this can't be right. You shot him!" I half shouted the last sentence, my eyes burning as confusion and betrayal swamped me. Mom's face was hard, her lips pressed together tight as she looked at me.

"Examinus punished her for that little blunder," Banks snarled. "When I saw you without the Hell-goat, I thought you'd failed, and decided to take matters into my own hands. The only reason your mother is still alive is that you subsequently led us straight to the book."

"Why?" Nox roared, startling me so much my daze lifted a little. "Why is he doing this?"

"He can tell you himself when he gets here."

Before I could draw a breath, the Hellhound pounced. Shadows burst from Nox, but rather than hit the Hellhound, they wrapped around me. I felt myself lifted from the ground and powered away, out of the path of the beast. It smashed into Nox, and they rolled across the floor as I came to a stumbling halt. I heard Banks start to chant, and tried to calm my panicked breathing and steady myself. The fire inside me roared up, raging and huge. It was as though it was rounding up my fear and confusion and betrayal and slamming them all into a locked cell in the back of my mind, where it couldn't affect me.

Fight or flight kicked in, hard.

And I was going to fight.

. . .

Just as I shoved my hand in my purse to get my crossbow, the sound of glass shattering rang out, followed by Francis screaming.

Leaving Nox wrestling with the flaming Hellhound, I turned and ran toward her and Claude. But my steps faltered before I even got halfway.

The glass in all the display cases lining the walls had shattered, and the heavy stone sarcophagi were sliding open. Sick fear crawled through me as I saw the first bandage-wrapped hand of a mummy groping toward us.

I heard Rory shout something behind me but couldn't make out the words for Francis' shrieking. Claude was trying to pull her away from the walls, where the mummies were, but she wouldn't move.

Behemoth was charging toward her and Claude, head-butting Francis' legs to get her moving. Her shrieking stopped as his horns made contact, she gave him a startled look, and then she was running toward me as fast as her frame would allow her.

"Rory's going for the book!" Behemoth said in my mind, as Francis barreled into me.

I caught her, looking over her shoulder to see a mummy lurching toward us, three more behind it.

I aimed the little crossbow, and felt it heat in my hand.

I fired.

The mummy heaved backward as a streaming bolt of gold light hit it, tearing through its shoulder. Bandages unfurled, revealing rotten dark skin beneath.

Another bolt of magic hit the one behind it, this one

made of black shadow, and I snapped my head to the left to see Claude aiming at them with his own crossbow.

"Beth, look!" Francis was tugging at my arm, and I fired again at an approaching mummy before turning.

Nox was still fighting with the enormous dog, only now, flames rose around them in a pattern. The symbol on Banks, I realized, staring.

Fear for Nox surged through me as the creature snapped and snarled at him, repeatedly shaking off his shadowy tendrils. The way Nox had dealt with the hellhound on the boat on the Thames was nothing like this fight. Was it because he was too weak? Or because this hellhound was different?

I saw Behemoth racing around the hellhound's heels, biting and ramming him whenever he got an opening.

I glanced behind us again, and fresh shudders of fear trickled through me. There were at least ten more mummies now, all climbing out of their coffins. One was hesitantly lifting an ancient weapon shaped like a scythe from a smashed display case. Claude shot it and it fell to the ground. I aimed my own weapon again and shot two that were closing in on our left, grimacing as their bandages unraveled. *Where the hell was Rory?*

"What do we do, what do we do, what do we—" Francis' frantic chanting was cut off abruptly as something skidded across the floor toward our feet. She screamed and I leaped backward before realizing what it was. A leather-bound book.

"Run!" Rory came sprinting toward us around the fire, Cornu right behind her.

I bent, scooping up the awkwardly heavy book, then froze as I straightened.

The sphinx was standing up.

The fifteen-foot-tall statue was rising onto its legs, the sound of stone cracking deafening.

"Nox!" I yelled.

"Run," he barked back. He was on top of the Hell-hound, but the flames were licking so high now that I could barely see more of him than the gold of his wings.

"I don't want to leave you!"

Rory and Cornu caught up to us, and I glimpsed Rory's burned dress and the soot on Cornu's face, before a burst of fire drew my attention back to Nox.

"Why can't he kill it?"

I could see fear in Rory's face for the first time. "I don't know. We have to get the book safe."

I held it out to her.

I wasn't leaving Nox. I knew it was stupid, danger-ous, and likely the wrong thing to do. But he was mine, and I wasn't leaving. "Go," I said. She hesitated a split second, before taking the book from me.

"I'll get help."

She sprinted past me, pink light glowing around her, and I aimed my little crossbow at the mummies she would need to get past to escape.

But suddenly she screamed, her body thrown into the air. I could do nothing as she zoomed over the fire, straight to Banks as though she were magnetized to him. He caught the book from her hand, and flicked his arm. She crashed hard into the side of the stone sphinx, and slid across the floor, stopping dangerously close to the flames.

"Enough!" Banks sounded gleeful as he roared the command. The mummies stilled and the flames around Nox and the Hellhound died down to embers abruptly.

Nox's shirt was singed and torn, and I could see blood on his temple. I started to move, but Banks' voice rang out again. "I said *enough*." His whole body was glowing yellow now, and I could swear he was a few feet taller. The great stone sphinx was huge beside him, my mom in front of it. The Collector was on his other side, his face almost white and his gaze fixed on the mummies behind us.

"Examinus needs more space for his welcome. We will move to the atrium," Banks announced.

"No! You can't do that!" The Collector sounded horrified, and Banks turned to him, a twisted smile on his face.

"I think you'll find, little man, that I can do anything I please."

He lifted his hand and the Collector convulsed. A shriek of agony burst from his mouth.

The Hellhound bounded from where it had crouched before Nox, and in one swift and lethal movement, tore the Collector's head from his shoulders.

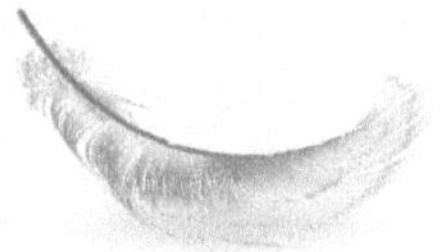

THIRTY

NOX

"There was supposed to be no killing!" Beth's mom yelled at Banks. Her eyes were full of hatred, and I was sure there was no allegiance between the two of them. Whether or not she had an allegiance with Examinus was another question.

Before Banks responded, Cornu ran toward him.

"It was you," the demon yelled, pointing at Banks but staring at the Collector's dead body. "You killed Madaleine, just the same way, with the beast. I saw her. Like this."

The Hellhound crouched low again, waiting for more orders, its nose twitching toward the spreading pool of blood.

"She was weak. Weaker than I thought she would be."

Cornu launched himself at Banks, screaming, and I threw my own power at the demon.

I got there just before Banks did, yanking him out of

the flash of yellow light that would have sent him back to Hell.

"That's enough, Banks! Fight me yourself, you fucking coward! Leave the hound out of it!"

Banks turned to me, eyes bright yellow as his magic poured from him.

"I don't even want to fight you now, you're so weak. That's why Madaleine was so easy to kill, I suppose. Her power was linked to yours. And you are so pathetic now."

Cornu roared from where my shadows kept him pinned to the floor, an anguished sound.

"Did you kill Madaleine for her sin page?"

"I thought she'd have the page on her," Banks shrugged. "And if she didn't, you'd get it back. You were always the last target."

Rage so hot I thought it might sear me from the inside out coursed through my body. "Did you kill her on Examinus' orders?"

"Examinus lets me operate as I wish. I've been feeding him information from the Ward for decades, so he knows he can trust me. When Max sold the book on, instead of bringing it back to him, Examinus gave me a chance to prove myself. He told me that if I could get more sin pages than you, he would make me the new Lord of Hell. But if you got your power back first, then you would keep the role."

"You failed," I snarled. "You managed to steal *one page* from a mortal man. Who you murdered for it."

Something flickered in his eyes, and he opened his mouth but closed it again. "The game's not over yet,

Lucifer. And Examinus agreed to level the playing field after the Sloth page. He gave me a little help, not just in the form of an accomplice." He glanced at Beth's Mom, then the yellow light roared up around him.

"He enhanced your power. And you're feeding it to the Hellhounds you're controlling." That was why I couldn't send the fucking creature back to Hell. I was fighting a god's power, not that of a lowly fucking angel and a wild beast from my own realm.

It made sense, when my mind cleared long enough to think rationally.

Examinus had lost his strongest weapon; me. So, when I made no move to act on my curse and retake my power and position for decades, he looked for someone else to take my place.

"What did Examinus promise you?"

"I will be Lord of Hell. You don't want the job, so why are you complaining?"

"You're a fucking lunatic. The Lord of Hell has unimaginable power, which should not be wielded by someone as emotionally unstable as you."

"Emotionally unstable? You literally gave your power to a mortal girl because you couldn't keep your dick in your pants. Does that sound emotionally stable to you?"

"I was created in a balance with my brothers. I am the only one able to keep the sin in the world at the right level."

"And what's the right level?" he asked me, his tone mocking. "Just enough to make sure people feel like they're living life? Just enough to fear authority? It's all bullshit."

"It's not bullshit. It's the way of life. It's how it's supposed to be."

"Well, it won't be, once Examinus and I take control."

I laughed, loud and long. "Examinus can't win a war. He is one god, and just as unhinged as you are."

"Fuck you, Lucifer. You've spent nearly a century shirking your responsibilities, and now you're telling me you're needed as part of a balanced world? You're a hypocrite."

He was right. I'd known for decades what I was doing to the balance. But I never planned to let the world fall to shit. And I sure as hell wouldn't allow whatever Examinus and this prick had planned to go ahead.

"Rather a hypocrite than psychopath."

"You know, you're a real disappointment. You're the devil. Lucifer. Lord of Hell, punisher of evil. And you're fucking dull. You fell in love with a plain, boring, mortal girl. What is wrong with you?"

My rage flared, and I clenched my fists, trying to contain it.

"I don't get what you see in her. Maybe, once I'm Lord of Hell, she'll go all swoony for me and I'll find out."

Fire burst across my skin. "Fucking touch her and I'll liquefy you," I roared, whirling toward him and launching as much power as I could directly at his chest. But it smashed into a wall of humming yellow light. The flames, flickering in the shape of a symbol around me, flared to life, and with a shot of agony that ran the full length of my spine, I felt my power slipping away.

"What—" I ground out, as my legs began to bend of their own accord.

"It's not just Hellhounds the symbol controls," Banks said gleefully. "I have you now, little Lucifer." His magic tightened around me, jerking me backward, so that I had to look at his face. "Don't worry, I won't kill her. I'll keep her."

"I will destroy Hell and everything in it before you even get close to her," I snarled through the pain.

"Lucifer, you can't even remove a Hellhound or get free from my bonds. I can't see you destroying Hell any time soon."

Pure hatred burned through my veins, poisoned with fear.

Beth was trapped in this place with me, along with all the people she cared about most.

THIRTY-ONE

BETH

If I got even the hint of a chance, I would kill Banks myself.

Nox's power inside me was a screaming rage, burning through my veins. I could actually tear the man apart.

"Time to go!" Banks sang out.

Nox was lifted high into the air and a path of fiery symbols lit up the hall, creating a passage between the exhibits. Nox's body flew from symbol to symbol as Banks walked alongside him.

I lifted my crossbow as he approached us, trying to keep it hidden from his view behind Francis.

There was a smell of something rotten, and I was grabbed from behind by something covered in fabric. My already unsettled stomach heaved when the overwhelming stench of the dead body inside the mummy bandages hit me. "Behemoth, check on Rory and Cornu," I gasped out, before a mummified hand closed over my mouth. Francis and Claude kicked and struggled as mummies grabbed them, but the creatures were too strong. Slowly, they dragged us along behind Banks and Nox.

"I'm with Rory. She's alive, but I can't wake her." The little goat's voice said in my mind. Relief tinged with anger came with his words.

"I'm sorry, Beth."

I tried to turn toward my mom's voice, but my captor had too tight a grip on my jaw.

"I'm doing this for your father. I have no choice. I didn't want others to die. But I have no choice."

I struggled harder, desperate to see her face, to see some sincerity in her eyes. I managed to jerk my head free long enough to turn to her, and was shocked to see tears in her eyes. I'd never seen her cry before. The mummy made a strangled moaning sound, then pulled my hair hard, jerking me backward. I yelped and heard Nox roar in response ahead of me.

"I'm sorry, Beth," she said again, as the mummies hand clasped back over my mouth. "Please, forgive me."

The mummies marched us all the way to the main atrium, where a burning symbol twenty feet high now danced on the central structure in the middle of the circular room. Within the flames I could see a swirling black and red vortex that looked familiar. It was what I'd seen behind Cornu, I realized, when he went to Hell.

In front of the symbol floated Nox, his golden wings stretched wide and his eyes black with shadow.

Gut deep fear surged through me on seeing him hanging there, trapped, offered up like some sort of sacrifice.

"I have created a portal worthy of you, Examinus!" Banks bellowed.

The symbol on the wall flashed a deep black, and a form emerged from it.

It was an enormous mass of sparking light in inky shadow for a split second, and then suddenly it was a man.

A huge man. Twenty-five feet tall, at least, with eyes like black gemstones. He had long black hair, and his body was on fire. Flames licked every part of his skin, as though they were clothes, obscuring details and giving off so much heat I thought I might suffocate.

Mercifully, the mummy dropped his hand from my mouth, and I sucked in air. I heard a small thump and turned to see the creature prostrate on the ground.

"Welcome, your holy one!" Bank sang delightedly. "We are ready!"

Examinus took a step toward Nox, who floated higher, so they were at eye level.

"I did warn you, Lucifer." The god's voice made my knees weak, it was so filled with power.

Nox growled. "This was not a fair fight."

"You had every opportunity."

"Banks is lying to you. I don't have all the sins. We have yet to find Pride."

Examinus laughed, and sound made me feel physically sick. "Pride was under your nose the entire time, Lucifer."

What?

"I'm no fool. When you carved up your power, I acted. I watched the angels you had chosen, and Pride was the obvious choice. I offered him a deal. I'd mask the sin power and disguise him as a Saint. And he would work for the Ward until I had need of him."

Banks.

Banks was Pride.

My heart hammered against my ribs as I stared at him, still glowing with magic, his eyes wild.

"I told you that you were clueless, Lucifer," Banks cackled. "All that time with me, and you never knew."

"You're nothing but a vessel for a god's power," Nox spat at him. "You have no power of your own."

Banks eyes hardened. "I will have all of your power, soon."

"Only an archangel can take my power. And they can only be created in balance with epic amounts of Heavenly magic." Nox bared his teeth at Banks and Examinus in turn. "I don't see either of my brothers here, offering up their services."

"I don't need your brothers. Not when I've got hundreds of Saints at my disposal, all brimming with the Heavenly magic I need."

Nox's face froze, and my own stomach flipped over.

Examinus turned his massive head to look at me. "Your mother has been a valuable asset to me. And your father is about to become one too."

"You said you would spare him!" My Mom's voice was shrill, and terror was etched into her face as she stared up at the huge flaming figure.

"I lied," Examinus hissed. "I will take every drop of magic I can get from the angels I have taken over the years, and their deaths will weaken my enemies further. I will enjoy every second of their demise."

"No!" Mom dropped to her knees, a sob ripping from her throat.

"You will start a war with your presence in London," shouted Nox, drawing the god's attention back to himself. "You know it is forbidden for you to be here."

Examinus stretched his arms wide, flames roaring up and down them, and smiled. "And what a way to start a war. With the creation of a new archangel, ready to destroy those who come to investigate my presence. This building will go down in history as the founding place of the new world."

THIRTY-TWO

BETH

My head was spinning, panic and fear overwhelming me. Examinus was going to use the Saints' magic to make a new archangel of Hell. And it would kill them all. Including my father.

I felt weak as the symbol behind Examinus flashed, then the swirling red and black intensified before turning translucent. There, on the other side of the portal, were cells. A long dark corridor, filled with barred doors stretched as far as I could see.

"Showtime!" cackled Banks.

Nox dropped to the floor suddenly, breaking his fall with a beat of his wings, and landing on one knee.

"Give me the sin pages," Banks said.

Nox stood slowly, and I saw his face as he turned.

Lethal fury was barely contained in his expression.

"Now," said Examinus, and Nox's face crumpled in pain, his wings convulsing.

I stepped forward, but my mom shot an arm out from

where she was still kneeling on the floor next to me. She gripped my shin, and shook her head when I looked down at her. Silent tears streamed from her eyes.

"I said now, Lucifer!"

Nox arched back, and I saw three small pieces of paper rise from his chest, as though torn from his skin. He let out an agonized groan, and hot tears streaked down my own cheeks.

The fire in my chest was raging, but I felt so utterly useless. I couldn't help Nox. I didn't know how to save my father.

Banks opened the Book of Sins, held it up, and the three pieces of paper flew toward it.

Nox slumped over, drawing in heavy breaths, and Banks pulled a piece of paper from his own pocket. The Pride page.

The book glowed with gold, and the pages settled.

"Lucifer. If you could do the honors." Banks stepped right up to him, holding the book.

"Never."

Examinus smiled again, the flames flickering on his skin. "I won't kill her, Lucifer," he said, and a searing heat enveloped me. My body lurched a little, then I was being lifted into the air. "I'll keep her. As my pet. Maybe Banks can play with her every now and then."

Terror ripped through me, and I kicked hard, trying to swing myself out of the invisible hold. But I was just lifted higher, closer to the gods massive face. Where Nox smelled like wood smoke, Examinus smelled like sulphur and burning chemicals, rotten and ancient.

"Put her down! I'll do it. Just let her live in London."

I started to fall, and instinct made me move my shoulders, my wings slowing my descent. I still landed hard, and it knocked the breath from me, but nothing hurt. I straightened as I tried to breathe.

"Do it."

A swirling white light burst from the portal, tendrils of fizzing magic bursting from every cell door and joining together to make one giant torrent of magic.

Nox looked at me, his eyes bursting bright blue for a split second, then he laid his hand on the book.

"No!" I heard my mom cry, and then Behemoth's voice rang in my mind.

"The only way to stop this is to stop the portal! Without the Saint's magic to offset it, Banks can't contain that much Hell magic."

I scrabbled to my feet. Nox was almost surrounded in shadow, and it was slowly pouring into the book through his hands, then trickling up Bank's arms as he clutched the other side of the book. Banks' face was one of pure ecstasy.

How could I stop the portal?

Behemoth charged toward me out of nowhere, his voice a hundred miles an hour in my head. "We have one shot. Channel your Hell magic. Are you ready?"

"Ready for what?" I half yelled, panic thrilling through me.

"My stone! Take my stone and concentrate all your magic into it!" The little goat morphed as I frantically pulled the stone from where it was secured in my bra strap. His horns grew first, gleaming gold, then his body matched, expanding and changing shape. Flames rippled across his black fur, huge fangs spread from his jaw, and his hooves sharpened into vicious claws.

With a roar, he leaped toward the portal. I gripped the stone, trying to channel everything that burned inside me into the gem. I pictured my dad in my head as I willed whatever Behemoth was trying to do to work with every single ounce of hope I possessed.

I had to save him. I'd come so far, my mom had given up so much. I couldn't fail now.

There was a bellow from above me, so loud I thought my skull might split. I did my best to concentrate on the stone, and I became aware of a darkness around me. The white light from the portal had stopped.

I looked up, dragging my attention from the stone, which was now so hot I could barely hold it. I got a glimpse of Behemoth, now as big as a Hellhound, standing on the other side of the portal like some unholy guard-dog, blocking the white light, before a scream drew my attention back to the hall.

The shadows were no longer flowing through the book and into Banks.

They were *consuming* him.

They flowed around him like a hurricane, tearing at his clothes and skin like they were full of razor blades.

"Examinus!" Banks screamed. His knees buckled, and he fell to the ground. Nox was growing, his wings expanding, glowing the brightest gold I had ever seen them. He closed both hands over the edges of the book, and when he spoke, the power made my dizzy.

"You are not worthy, Banks. You are not worthy. Your Pride made you believe you were able to contain my massive power. And you were wrong. You believed you were above retribution, able to kill at your leisure. You will be punished accordingly."

I tore my gaze from them to look up at Examinus, expecting him to do something. But the god was still, nothing but his flames moving as he watched.

There was an explosion of gold light, and it rushed into Banks' kneeling form, the shadows expelled in a heartbeat. His body arced into the air, the golden light holding it up as it rose. When all the light had entered his body, he drifted back to the ground.

Slowly, he straightened. His eyes burned with light, and his cruel smile spread across his face.

"You were wrong, Lucifer," he said, but then he froze. A beam of gold burst through his cheek, followed by a stream of shadows. Another beam erupted on his neck, then hundreds more started to shoot from his chest, all followed by tendrils of shadows. He screamed, and I saw the shadows burning his skin as they poured from him, dark, congealed blood leaking from the holes left behind.

The power was tearing him apart from the inside.

My own knees gave out as I felt the power of the sins flowing around the room, free and uncontained, killing the angel they were escaping from.

I closed my eyes, desperately drawing in breath. One

second, I was so angry I wanted to kill, the next, so hungry I thought I would throw up.

My brain cycled through every sin, poison Envy believing everyone was better than me, unbearable Sloth making me want to give up on everything, lethal Pride trying to convince me that I could take on a god and win.

I gasped for air, pulling on the power inside me to ease the pain in my head, the draw of the sins.

I forced my eyes open to see Nox's wings larger than I'd ever seen them, and all the gold light and shadowy power flowing into them. All I could see of Banks was a charred and bloody mess on the ground.

"Lucifer," hissed Examinus. "I underestimated you. And overestimated Banks. You are the true Lord of Hell."

Nox beat his wings, lifting from the ground and turning to face Examinus.

My breathing stopped completely at the sight of him.

His skin shone like the stone in my hand, flashing a shimmering onyx as he moved. He had horns as gold as his wings, and power flowed around him in a storm.

He looked like the trinity painting. A divine, mighty force, unparalleled. Death and fear and pain, in the most beautiful package in existence.

I knew, as I stared, that the curse was lifted. All of his power was returned.

The heat in my chest flared.

All his power was returned, except the tiny ball inside me.

In unison, Examinus and Nox turned to face me.

"Take what is yours, Lucifer, and win this war with

me," Examinus boomed. "Your brothers are on their way. They sense my presence here. Take back what you left in this mortal girl, and let us be glorious in our victory."

"Never."

The fire covering Examinus leaped, and Nox beat his wings, hovering in front of the massive god. "You still defy me?"

"You need me, Examinus. Here is your proof that only I can be what you need me to be." Nox gestured at Banks' remains. "I propose we make a deal."

Examinus stared at Nox, fury in his cruel, ethereal face. "You dare speak to me like an equal?"

He roared and grew another ten feet. The glass roof of the building shattered, and I threw my arms over my head as the shards rained down over us. "You forget, child, I own you! And now your power resides in her, I own her too!"

My body jerked, and I found myself standing, then striding toward the fallen Book of Sins. I fought against the movement, but it was futile. Panic spread through me as I was forced forward, able to do nothing. Nox flew toward me but seemed to roll at the last minute, as though someone had pulled a string behind him, sending him crashing to the floor. My body turned, and I ducked to pick up the book. I squeezed my eyes closed as they met the fallen body of Banks.

"I may not be able to force you to give up your power, but I am still a god!"

I spun, utterly unable to control my own movements, and saw Nox moving awkwardly toward me, strain and anger in every line of his face. Like unwilling puppets, we fought uselessly against him as he drew us together.

"Take back your power, Lucifer," Examinus hissed as Nox gripped the book. "Either take back what you gave her, or I kill the Saints."

Dad. All those innocent angels.

"Take it," I hissed to Nox. "I don't need it."

"Then what?" Nox yelled, his eyes fixed on me, but the question clearly for Examinus.

"Then, we kill your brothers."

"No."

"Then the angels die."

I heard a chittering, then a wail. I tried to turn my head to look at the portal, but I didn't need to. I flinched as Behemoth was thrown across the room behind Nox.

He was no longer guarding the portal.

Shadows swirled around Nox, and fear filled his blue eyes. His body began to glow.

"What's happening?"

Examinus started laughing, and my head swam.

"Beth, my power... It's moving."

Nox was right. The light and shadow were pouring into the book, as they had with Banks. Slowly, a shadowy tendril licked from the book, over my skin.

"Why is this happening?" Even over the sound of Examinus' laughter, I sounded frantic.

"I don't know. I don't know." I had never seen Nox look scared. But at that moment, sheer terror took his features.

"You are drawing his power!" Examinus glee echoed

through the room. "How perfect! Lucifer kills the woman he loves with the power he doesn't want!"

I was going to end up like Banks.

My blood turned to ice in my veins at the realization.

A tendril of shadowy magic crawled up my arm, and a burst of power lit me up, making my breath catch. Heat tingled through me. The gold light began to flow from the book into me, pleasure, excitement, power and strength all rushing through me. I tried to force it back, used every single bit of strength I had, both physical and mental, to repel the magic. But it kept coming.

I had minutes before all the power flowed into me.

Nox's voice was filled with as much terror as his face was, his words blurring together, frantic. "Beth, I'm so sorry, Beth, I can't stop it, I can't—"

"I love you." I cut him off, saying the words as clearly as I could through my tears. "Nox, I love you. I regret nothing." It was true. "I would rather die today, filled with your strength, than live a hundred lifetimes never feeling what you make me feel. You've changed me, brought out my very best. I love you. Save my parents. Please, please try to save them."

"Beth, I can't lose you. I can't."

"Please."

He stared at me, his eyes bright. So beautiful. I would make sure they were the last thing I saw.

"I love you," he choked. A single tear rolled down his cheek. "Beth—"

The power filling me now was so strong that my body

was tensing, and it was becoming painful. Shadow and light was beginning to churn around me.

"Beth!" The voice wasn't Nox's. It was my mom's, and she was sobbing. "I'm sorry, I should have warned you!"

I felt something cold on my neck, then a snap, as the necklace was yanked from my throat.

Abruptly, the shadows swirling around me cleared and rushed back to Nox. The light stopped flowing into me, the overwhelming feelings no longer crushing me. I blinked through tears, relief and confusion making my vision hazy.

But I saw my mom, clutching the ruby necklace.

I tried to move, but I was still under the god's control, my limbs not my own.

"The necklace is like a genie's lamp," Mom blurted out as Examinus began to roar. "It's the only thing that can trap Examinus! Beth, we have to get the necklace to touch him, it's the only way!"

Her face changed as all of a sudden her body was flung up into the air. Examinus roared a laugh.

"Puny little human!" he bellowed.

Distracted by my mom, his grip over my body lessened a little.

"Beth, if that necklace is what she says it is..." Hope flared in Nox's eyes and his voice was urgent. "It must have been drawing my power to you. There's no humanity in Examinus, he's pure power. If we can get that necklace on him... He'll be trapped."

I heard mom scream a single word. My father's name.

I pushed against the power holding me, trying to make my hands release their grip on the book. I felt Nox do the same, and then the Book of Sins crashed to the floor between us.

Nox grabbed my hand and ran toward Examinus. The god flicked his flaming hand, and mom's body flew through the air in time with him, like a toy.

"Beat your wings," Nox called to me.

"I thought you said I couldn't fly!"

"You've taken a lot of my power, Beth. Try."

I moved my shoulders and gasped as my feet immediately left the floor. Nox pulled me higher, and I pictured my wings, willing them to beat harder.

They did.

"I'll distract him, but I won't be able to fight him for long. Get to your mom and get the ruby to touch him."

"Okay," I gasped.

Nox let go of my hand and roared. "Face me, Examinus!"

His skin flashed, and power burst from him, directed straight at Examinus' face. I spun in the air, heading for my mom as Examinus bellowed.

"Mom!" I grabbed her waist, trying to yank her from the power holding her as I flew. There was a slight resistance, then I heard more roaring and felt a blast of Nox's power. Mom became heavy in my grip for a split second, then strength surged through me, making my muscles feel like they were swelling.

"The necklace, Beth! We must get the necklace to him!"

I banked and flew straight at the god's throat.

~

I got within a foot and crashed into an invisible barricade. I tried to push through, but it was like beating against a brick wall. An unfathomably *hot* brick wall.

Power was blasting around us, Nox swooping and diving behind us as I tried to push through the barrier of magic around Examinus. I could feel Nox's magic in me, no longer a ball of fire in my chest, but flowing through my whole body, keeping my wings beating. I felt another burst of heat, then Behemoth's voice spoke in my mind. "We're here."

I threw a glance over my shoulder. On the ground behind us was Behemoth, Rory and Cornu. Behemoth and Cornu were emitting dark glows, and Rory a bright pink one, all focused on me.

They were adding their power to mine.

It was almost enough. But not quite.

"Nox! Help me!"

In a heartbeat, Nox was behind me, and he launched a blast of pure golden light at Examinus' throat.

The resistance vanished, and I lurched forward, crashing into his flaming skin. Mom screamed as the flames licked over us, but threw her arm out, slamming the necklace onto his giant neck.

There was a blast so strong my vision turned completely black, and I was catapulted backward. I was so dazed I didn't even register letting go of my mom. I heard someone screaming my name and tried to shake my head.

I was falling.

I beat my wings, tipping in the air, trying to right myself, then felt hard tiles slam into my body.

I lifted my head, utterly disorientated, my hip in so much pain I could hardly breathe.

Nox was in the air, my mom limp in his arms.

And Examinus...

Examinus was disappearing into a swirling ball of sparking energy, the ruby necklace gleaming bright in the center of the mass. He was being sucked into it, like a damn genie into a lamp. An awful wailing sound burst from his ethereal form, and I gasped at the pain it caused in my head. I blinked once more, then my vision blacked out completely.

THIRTY-THREE

BETH

"Beth? Beth, wake up."

"Move."

"No, give her some space."

"Her wings are big. Like, really big."

The voices filtered in and out of my hearing as I struggled to stay conscious.

Nothing hurt, I just couldn't stay awake long enough to make sense of what was happening around me.

I felt warmth, then someone touch their hands to my face.

My eyes flickered open.

"Nox?" I breathed. His blue eyes shone bright with relief as they focused on me.

"Beth."

He leaned down, pressed his lips to mine, and the fogginess vanished.

We were alive. We were alive, and he was kissing me.

I moved back, and he helped me to sit up. Behemoth

was right beside me, and he gave me a gentle head-butt. Rory stood behind him, a wad of fabric pressed against her head, her dress stained with blood. Francis sat on the floor a few feet from me, fanning her face and beaming at me whilst Claude stood protectively beside her.

I stared around the room.

All that was left of the flames were dark embers. Gabriel stood over my mom, who had her head between her knees. Michael was in the middle of the room, holding the ruby necklace like it was about to bite him. Shattered glass covered everything.

"What happened?"

I blinked at Nox, and he ran his hand softly along my jaw. "Your Mom saved us. It's over. The ruby was enchanted by a djinn, just like Behemoth's stone."

"He's... in the necklace?"

"Yes."

"How did Mom know?"

"I'm not sure. Gabriel is healing her."

I scrabbled to get up. "Healing? Is she okay?"

Nox rubbed his hand up my arm soothingly as he steadied me on my feet. "She'll be fine. She got burned pretty bad."

"How... How am I not hurt?"

Nox's gaze flicked over my shoulders. "You got a lot of my power, before your mom got the necklace off you. I think it suits you better than the ruby."

I stared at him.

He was right.

I could feel it. Not a little ball of feisty fire any more.

A torrent of strength, flowing through my body, clearing the fatigue and confusion.

"Is that why I could fly? And carry Mom?"

He nodded. "Yes."

"But I'm human. I'm not an angel."

"Beth, I'm not sure what you are now." He pulled me to him, pushing my hair back from my face. "Except that you are mine."

"Always," I whispered, and he kissed me again. Love flowed through the contact, pure joy that he was safe and we were together flooding me as powerfully as the new magic. "I meant every word I said," I whispered. "Every word."

"I know. I love you."

"I'm sorry to break this up." Michael's voice cut across the moment. White light shone bright around his hands, and the necklace had vanished. "But we need to talk. If what Lucifer says is true, then there are hundreds of angels that need rescuing. I would like to check the truth of this claim sooner rather than later."

Mom's head snapped up from where she was sitting. "George," she croaked.

Dad.

"Do you know where they're being kept?" Gabriel asked her gently.

"She can't tell you. She has a tongue-tying curse," said Nox.

"Can Gabriel not lift it?" I asked.

"No. Or we'd have been able to do so with Max."

Cornu stepped forward, avoiding Michael's face

completely. "I recognized the place we saw in the portal. Its magical signature."

"Really?" Nox raised his eyebrows at him.

"Yes. I believe it is the caves under my family's fortress."

"Thank you, Cornu," I breathed.

Nox looked at me, face filled with concern. "I must go. My brothers can't enter Hell. Will you be alright?"

I nodded. "Yes. Save my father."

He kissed me one more time, then looked at Cornu. "Will you come with me?"

The demon hesitated, then nodded. "You could have sent me back to Hell. But you let me stay."

"You deserved your retribution. I respected Madaleine. And I'm sorry for her loss."

Cornu tipped his chin, his stance straightening. "Let us go to Hell and find these angels."

As soon as Nox and Cornu had left, I made my way to my mom.

"Beth," she breathed as I dropped down to the tiles beside her. "Beth, I can't begin to tell you how sorry I am." Tears spilled from her eyes. "About everything."

I glanced up at Gabriel, and he smiled. "Her skin is healed. She will be fine," he said, then turned, leaving us alone.

I leaned in, wrapping my arms around her as tightly

as I could. "You saved us all. Me, Dad, possibly the whole of humanity. You were so brave."

"No," she sobbed into my shoulder. "I was weak. I did everything he told me to do, and it got people killed."

"You also did a bunch of shit he didn't tell you to do, and it was down to you that we defeated him!" I leaned back, wiping tears from my normally stoic, unemotional mother's face. Relief poured through me, and the desire to just hold her for hours was intense.

I pulled her back to me, and she let me.

"How did you know about the necklace?"

"Your father worked for the Ward many years go. When Examinus first sent me to London, I got in touch with one of your father's old friends there, and he smuggled me into the archives at Ward HQ. I went through everything they had to find anything that could kill a god. I soon discovered that killing him wasn't an option, but I might be able to trap him. I found three or four objects that were strong enough and when I saw one of them was for sale here...it was the best chance I had."

"So that's who you were talking to when I heard you on the radio." She turned against my shoulder, blinking watery eyes at me as her eyebrows raised in question. "I heard you telling someone that I could never find you."

Guilt washed over her face. "I didn't want you involved. But then Banks started getting impatient, and Examinus threatened to kill your father... I had to send you the note with the museum ticket. I hid the symbol in there too, just in case it would help you. I'm sorry Beth."

"It's okay, Mom. You were amazing."

"You really think so?"

"Yes."

She fell silent a moment. "You were amazing too," she said quietly. "When I saw you had the power of the devil in you, I was heartbroken. But now..." She moved awkwardly, so that she was facing me. "Now I see how strong you really are. And from what I've seen of you the past few days, I do not believe you are changed by him."

"I am changed by him, Mom. But not for the worse. I swear."

Her eyes filled up again. "There is so much of your father in you. I have missed you both, so much."

I felt my own eyes grow hot. "I know, Mom. Me too."

There was a noise behind us, and Michael spoke. "They are coming."

I stood up quickly, pulling Mom up too, as a small, swirling portal appeared on the other side the destroyed atrium.

Nox and Cornu stepped through it, each holding the arm of a man. A man I'd not seen in five years.

My dad.

"Gloria, Beth!" His voice was barely a whisper, but it was so filled with joy it carried to us all the same.

"George!" My Mom was running and my eyes blurred with tears as I followed her. Mom flung her arms around him, and Nox and Cornu stepped away. I looked into dad's face as he pulled my Mom tight to him.

He looked just the same. Warmth oozed from his

face, laugh lines wrinkling his skin in all the right places. He stroked Mom's hair as she sobbed, speaking softly to her. "It's okay, Gloria, I'm here. I'm here."

He locked his eyes on mine as I reached them, and the lump escaped my throat in a sob of my own. "Beth," he said, beaming at me. "I knew you'd come through. I knew you'd find us. I always knew. I always knew my girl would save us."

"Okay. So why did you want to talk to me?" I looked between the three archangels and my mom and dad. Behemoth chittered.

If you'd told a younger version of me that my mom would ever be sipping tea on the devil's couch, I would have told you that you were crazy. But that was, in fact, exactly what was happening.

We were in Nox's drawing room. A number of surprising things had come out of the showdown at the museum, not least of which was that Nox had allowed both of his brothers into his house to discuss the running of Hell. Along with my parents, for some reason.

One of the other surprising things was Behemoth's official request to Techa to become my Guardian. I was pretty sure he'd made up the role of Guardian, *capital G*, but to my sheer delight, Techa had humored him. Behemoth and I were a permanent fixture, and my heart warmed every time I remembered that. He'd been a massive part of saving my dad's life, guarding the Saints through the portal like he had.

Also, he really was cute.

"Beth, we've had more tests result back from Nina, and I've spoken extensively to Adstutus. None of them know why my power has been able to stay in your body. But you're not human anymore. And you're not an angel."

"I'm not human?" I repeated. I'd had enough time to get used to the wings and the magic heat that my body now produced for that statement to be less alarming than it might have been. But it was still pretty unsettling. "What am I?"

"We don't know, and that's very exciting," said Michael. I looked at him in surprise. His usually chilly reception to Nox had vanished since the Saints were rescued, and he was beaming at me. His joy was infectious.

"Exciting?"

"Yes," Nox said. "I believed that the only way to carve up my power was to put it into Hell creatures. Fallen angels strong enough to contain it. But, as you saw, it corrupted them all."

"Except Madaleine. She was strong enough," I interrupted.

"I'm not sure it did her any good," mused Gabriel.

"Not the point," said Nox, looking seriously at everyone. "The point is that whatever you are, Beth, you can carry my power. Without corruption."

I blinked at him. "How?"

"We're assuming it's to do with you being the offspring of an angel. Not just any angel. A Saint. The dormant good in you can offset the Hell magic."

"Does this mean you might be able to share your role after all?" I couldn't keep the excitement from my voice as I looked at Nox.

He nodded, eyes bright. "Perhaps. I think I gave my power to the wrong types of angel."

"There is a problem though," interjected Michael. We all looked at him. "You're *not* an angel. Which means you can't be given a position in the Veil, manage sin magic, or be useful in any way. Because you won't live long enough."

The abruptness of Michael's words, delivered so cheerily, hit me in the gut.

"I think this is where I come in." My dad's deep, rumbling voice drew all our attention to him. He raised his eyebrows at Nox, and Nox grinned.

"Your father has been helping me the last couple of days. With this." Nox leaned down and slid a small leather-bound book out from under the couch. He laid it on the coffee table in front of us.

"What is it?" I breathed.

"A new book of sins. Except, not for sins. This moves Heavenly magic."

"You made something for Heavenly magic?" I looked at his brothers, expecting them to react. But Gabriel was smiling, relaxed, and Michael was leaning froward eagerly.

"You all knew about this," I said slowly.

"Yes. We didn't tell you, because we didn't want to get your hopes up until we knew it would work," dad said gently.

"What would work?"

Dad reached out, taking my hand. "Beth, if you'll let me, I'd like to give you some of my magic."

Tears sprang to my eyes immediately, and I squeezed his hand back, hard. "Really?"

"Yes. If you want it."

"Of course I want it! I would do anything to be more like you." I leaned forward, hugging him hard, and he laughed.

"Beth, there's something you need to know first," Nox said. His face was serious, but excitement was dancing in his eyes when I turned to him. "Malc and Adstutus think that combining Hell and Heavenly magic within you will turn you into something new. An angel, but not Fallen or Saint. The first of your kind."

"Immortal?" I whispered.

"Yes." His voice dropped, low and husky. "Able to be by my side for eternity."

"I'll do it."

"Here we go," dad said, and picked up the book. He shifted in his seat and opened the book. The scrawl on the pages was beautiful, though I understood none of it.

He turned a few, then stopped, putting his finger on one with a small sketch in the middle of a daisy. Carefully, he tore the page from the book. Pale blue light shone briefly, and he set the book down on the couch between us.

He smiled at me. "This is going to work. I know it is. And I couldn't be happier to share my power with you, my love," he said.

With a deep breath, he offered me the page, and began to speak in Latin. I took it and gasped as power tingled up my arm, spreading fast.

Hope. There was no other way to describe the feeling as it swept through my body, twirling and entwining with the fierce passion that now burned so steadily.

Hope.

That I would be the first of my kind. A bridge between Nox and his brothers. A way for him to share his epic role with those who could carry it out fairly.

Hope.

That I would be able to spend an eternal life with him. I would be able to keep him whole, keep his soul true. And he would be able to spend an endless life filling me with that limitless, fantastical pleasure of mind, body and soul.

Dad beamed at me around the words he spoke, and then he let go of the page. It glowed again, that same pale blue, and I knew I was connected to it. Forever.

"How do you feel?" mom whispered, when dad stopped speaking.

"I feel... Good. Hopeful," I grinned.

Dad leaned forward, kissing me on the cheek.

Michael stood up. "When you have seen the genie,

and he can confirm that you have become an angel, we will return." He turned to Nox, and Nox stood up too. "Until then, we will start looking for suitable candidates to rotate responsibility of your sins, brother."

Nox nodded his head once. "Thank you."

Michael gave one last beaming smile to everyone in the room, then strode out the door. Gabriel clasped Nox's hand. "See you soon, brother," he grinned, and followed Michael.

"Well," Mom said. "What do we do now?"

Behemoth jumped up onto the seat that Gabriel had vacated. "This is a momentous occasion. We should do something momentous."

"Like what?"

My phone rang before anyone could answer. I pulled it from my pocket. A video call. From Francis.

"Sweetie!"

"Hi Francis. I'm with Nox and my parents," I said quickly, before she could say anything inappropriate. I turned the camera around and everyone waved at her. She waved wildly back.

"Look who I'm with!" She moved her phone so that more than just her face filled it. Standing behind her, one perfect eyebrow raised, was Rory.

"Oh! Hi!"

"She's been teaching me some moves. With my honey's crossbow," Francis explained.

She had gotten over being attacked by living mummies and seeing a man have his head ripped off by a Hellhound remarkably quickly. Claude had reported that within a few hours of getting her safely home from the ordeal at the museum, she had told six of the old folks the entire story, eaten most of a leftover cake, and passed out. The next morning, she tried to convince everyone she'd told that it was an idea for a film she was pitching. Whenever she had spoken to me about it, her eyes lit up with excitement.

I suspected she was learning to use the crossbow as a reason to spend more time with Claude, rather than through any fear for her life.

"That's great," I told her.

"It is. We were wondering if you wanted to have dinner tonight. Here at the home. They're showing The Matrix in the rec room."

I looked up at Nox, hiding my smile. The idea of the devil having dinner in an old folks' home would never not be a little amusing.

"Why don't we have dinner here? We can watch the Matrix in my home cinema. And someone other than the retirement home chef can cook," he added under his breath.

Francis beamed at him. "Honestly, I was kinda hoping you'd say that."

When she'd rung off, mom and dad stood up. "You would be welcome for dinner too," Nox said, a little awkwardly.

Dad smiled. "Great. We have to pick up some furniture for the apartment, so we'll come back over about seven?"

"See you then."

~

As soon as we'd waved them off in a taxi, Nox turned to me, growling. "I thought they'd never all leave."

Desire was dancing in his eyes, and I could feel his Lust power whispering over my skin, setting my pulse racing.

"You want me alone, Mr. Nox?"

"I want you, period." He stepped into me, pressing me hard against the wall of the hallway.

Liquid need pooled between my legs as his hot body made contact with mine.

Gently, tantalizingly gently, he brushed his thumb over my cheek, then my lip.

"This is us, Beth. If you want it to be. This can be the life we live."

Joy pulsed through my body as I stared up at his utterly beautiful face. "Yes. I want it. I want you. I want this life."

"Tell me you're mine."

"I'm yours."

"I love you, Miss Abbott."

"I love you, Mr. Nox."

THE END

Thank you so much for reading The Devil's Deal, I hope you enjoyed it! If so I would be eternally grateful for a review! They help so much; just click here and leave a couple words, and you'll make my day :)

This series is a departure from what I usually write - which is Greek mythology based romantic fantasy - and I wanted to say thank you so much for giving it a chance!

I was taken by surprise by just how much I missed London when lockdown and the pandemic struck, and after a few months at home, these characters and this world were demanding to be written - my existing schedule be damned!

This last year has been hard for everyone I know, and my own family was no exception - and that resulted in the writing of this series slowing down after the initial rush. I hope you are as happy with the end of Beth and Nox's story as I am, and **thank you so much** for waiting as long as you have for it.

I will be returning to Olympus with my next series, The Poseidon Trials, but this is not the last you'll see of the Veil (Francis, Rory and Behemoth have some adventures to go on and, quite frankly, there's no way I can stop them.)

ACKNOWLEDGMENTS

Special thanks to my mum and my husband, for *everything* the last year. Just, everything.

Thank you to my amazing editor, without whom this book would probably not have been finished until 2025.

And thank you so much to my author friends who have kept me sane and happy and motivated when not a lot else did. You know who you are - thank you! xxx